Ciro Alegría

CIRO ALEGRÍA was born in the province of Huamachuco in Peru on November 4, 1909. When he was three his parents moved to a ranch on the banks of the Marañón River, where he first came to know the agrarian people of Peru, and where he first heard their tales and legends. At the age of seven he was sent to school in the city of Trujillo, one of his teachers being the gifted poet César Vallejo. In 1930 he entered the University of Trujillo, but his participation in the struggle against the dictatorship which governed his country prevented him from continuing his studies. One of the founders of the Aprista party, he was imprisoned for his political activities on different occasions and finally exiled to Chile in 1934. There he worked as a journalist and writer. *The Golden Serpent*—a revised and expanded version of his short story *The Raft*—won first prize in a novel contest sponsored by the publishing house of Nascimento of Santiago, Chile. In 1936, his health weakened by political activities and by the rigors of prison life and exile, Alegría entered a tuberculosis sanitarium, where he remained for two years. During his convalescence he wrote *The Hungry Dogs;* this second novel received first prize in a contest sponsored by another Santiago publisher. In 1941, his *Broad and Alien Is the World* won a $5,000 award for the best Latin American novel from Farrar & Rinehart in New York. That year he visited the United States; during World War II he worked for the Office of War Information and the Coördinator of Inter-American Affairs. More recently the author has taught at the University of Puerto Rico.

The Golden Serpent

by
CIRO ALEGRÍA

Translated, and with an Afterword,
by Harriet de Onís

A SIGNET CLASSIC

Published by the New American Library

A timeless treasury of the world's great writings.

Signet Classics are especially selected and handsomely

designed for the living library of the modern reader.

COPYRIGHT, 1943, BY FARRAR & RINEHART, INC.

AFTERWORD COPYRIGHT © 1963 BY THE NEW AMERICAN LIBRARY
OF WORLD LITERATURE, INC.

All rights reserved. No part of this book may be reproduced in any
form without permission from the publisher. For information
address Holt, Rinehart and Winston, Inc., 383 Madison Avenue,
New York 17, New York.

Reprinted by arrangement with Holt, Rinehart and Winston, Inc.,
who have authorized this softcover edition.

First Printing, March, 1963

SIGNET TRADEMARK REG. U.S. PAT. OFF. AND FOREIGN COUNTRIES
REGISTERED TRADEMARK—MARCA REGISTRADA
HECHO EN CHICAGO, U.S.A.

SIGNET CLASSICS are published by
The New American Library of World Literature, Inc.
501 Madison Avenue, New York 22, New York

PRINTED IN THE UNITED STATES OF AMERICA

Contents

1

The River, the Men,
and the Rafts

Where the Marañón breaks through the mountains in a determined forward advance, the Peruvian highland is as ferocious as a mountain lion at bay. It is no place to be caught off guard.

When the river rises it roars against the cliffs, spreading out over the wide banks and covering the pebbled beaches. It rushes along boiling, roaring through gaps and bends, gliding through the open stretches, slimy and yellow with fertile silt whose penetrating smell bespeaks its powerful germinal force. In February, when the river swells to its greatest height, the air all around is filled with a throbbing reverberation, and one is in awe of this turbulent stream and heeds its roar as a personal warning.

We, the *cholos* (half-breeds) of the Marañón, listen to its voice with an alert ear. We know not where it rises or where it ends, this river which would kill us if we tried to measure it with our rafts, but it tells us plainly of its immensity.

Its waters rush by, dragging along masses of debris that reach from one bank to the other. Tree trunks that twist and writhe like bodies; branches, brush, stones, all travel along in a shapeless mass, imprisoning

7

everything that crosses their path. God help the raft that gets caught in one of these jams! It is dragged along until it is finally flung against a jutting cliff or swallowed up by a whirlpool, along with the jumble of logs, as though it were some worthless bit of trash.

When the boatmen see them coming, black against the water, they row like mad downstream, until they can land on some friendly bank. At times they do not judge the distance well as they cut across and they are caught by one end of the jam. Sometimes, too, if the logs are partly submerged they do not see them until they are almost on them, and then they have to trust to luck. They drop their paddles—those wide oars that raise the water as though they were going to swallow it—cinch their flannel pants tighter and either hop from log to log or dive out of their way until they come up or are lost for good.

The heavy skies of the rainy season unleash wild storms which fall upon and tear at the slopes of the mountains and digging still deeper furrows in the earth, rush down to our Marañón. The river is a world of yellow mud.

We *cholos* whose story this is live in Calemar. We know many other valleys which have been formed where the hills have retreated or been eaten away by the river, but we do not know how many there are upstream or how many there are downstream. We do know that they are all beautiful and they speak to us with their haunting, ancestral voice which is strong like the voice of the river.

The sun sparkles on the red cliffs that form the gorge and rise until it seems as though they were piercing the canopy of the sky, which is sometimes leaden with clouds and sometimes as light and blue as a bit of percale. Below spreads the valley of Calemar and the river does not cut through it but skirts it on one side, lapping the base of the cliffs in front of it. Two footpaths, showing white against the rocks, twisting and turning like a pair of drunken dancers, lead down to this cliff-walled spot.

The paths are narrow but they are all man and beast need to travel these steep familiar mountains whose steps, windings, abysses and passes are known even during the night to well-trained country senses. The road is but a ribbon that marks the way and man and beast follow it calmly, to the sound of pebbles crunching underfoot, in sun, rain or darkness.

One of the paths begins alongside the river, at the foot of the crags, goes panting part way up a yellow slope where leafy *pate* trees grow, and loses itself in the shadows of a gap between the hills. It is that way that strangers come to us and we go to the fairs of Huamachuco and Cajabamba, taking coca to sell there, or just for the fun. We of the valley are rovers by nature, perhaps because the river—a new God—fashioned us out of the water and clay of the world.

The other comes down from the highlands of Bambamarca, along the gap of a ravine, whose waters sing as they sparkle under the cliffs, and are in as much of a hurry to reach the Marañón as the road itself. Both disappear amidst the shady foliage of the valley, the path merging with a lane lined with plum trees, while the water runs into the flumes which water our gardens and give us our drinking water. Down this road come the Indians who whimper over their mosquito bites and think they hear snakes crawling all night long, as though they had spread their blankets over a snake hole. They come to trade potatoes, *ollucas,* or the other things they raise in the highlands for coca, red pepper, bananas and the many fruits this place abounds in.

They do not eat mangos, plums or guavas, because they think they give them malaria. In spite of this, and though they merely come here and go right back, they get the chills and fevers and die shivering like dogs in the wind in their huts which tremble at the blasts of the highland gales. This is not a land of Indians, and only a few have managed to acclimate themselves. To the Indians the valley is like a feverish agitation and to us half-breeds, the loneliness and the silence of the

highlands make our breasts ache. Here we flourish like
the green bay tree.

Life is beautiful here. Even death nourishes life in its
bosom. In the cemetery, which rests behind a slope from
which a little church looks out upon the valley with
the single eye of its white belfry, the crosses can hardly
stretch out their arms, such is their voluptuous abandon.
They are shaded by orange trees which are laden with
deliciously sweet fruit. That is what death is like here.
And when the river swallows someone, it does not
matter. We know that it is our enemy, and there is an
old song which shows that we enjoy the risks we take:

> River Marañón, let me cross.
> You are strong and powerful,
> You never forgive.
> River Marañón, I have to cross.
> You have your waters,
> I, my heart.

But life always triumphs. Man is like the river, deep,
having his ups and downs, but always stout-hearted.
The earth rejoices in the abundance of its fruits, and
nature is a riot of color, all its rich shades of green
contrasting with the bright red of the rough crags and
the blue and milky white of the rocks and the sand of
the banks.

Coca fields, banana and yucca plantings grow in the
shadow of alligator pear, guava, orange and mango
trees, through which the wind soughs voluptuously,
spreading the fertile pollen.

The trees entwine and sway in an unending dance.
Hundreds of birds, drunk with life, sing in the shade of
the groves, and farther off beside the cliffs under the
gold of the sun are the pasture fields where the horses
and donkeys that carry our loads fatten. The light
glistens on their sleek backs and their pulsing veins
stand out in ramiform design on their legs. Every whin-
ny is a hymn of rejoicing.

The houses, of woven-reed walls and banana frond roofs, drowse among the trees beside the gardens. They stand straight for they are built around slender *sinamomo* poles. Out of them come the *cholos,* with spade, pick or axe in hand, on their way to some task, or with only the lime gourd, to stretch out and do nothing as they chew their coca under a mango or a friendly cedar while the air shimmers in the sun.

For it must be known that the tree our axes always spare is the cedar, and strangers gaze in openmouthed amazement at the abundance of them. Once in a while somebody in a good humor cuts one down and, with an adze, hacks out a little table or a bench. But most frequently they are to be found standing, spreading their broad shade over houses and hills, paths and flumes, and, naturally, over any person who seeks it.

The most highly prized tree is the balsa. Ash gray in color, this favorite grows at a snail's pace and belongs to the owner of the place where it grows. Who ever heard of fighting over an alligator pear or an orange tree, or even a cedar? Nobody. But a balsa tree is a different matter. There have been serious fights, with knife play and blood. Once the *cholo* Pablo killed Martín for having cut down a balsa tree of his while he was away. Pablo came back from town, missed his tree, and began to ask questions. He went straight over to see Martín who was sitting at the door of his cabin.

"Who cut down my tree?"

And the *cholo* Martín, looking as innocent as a lamb, smiled: "Did someone cut it down?"

Pablo tightened his belt, getting ready to fight, and answered: "Of course somebody cut it down. It didn't walk off by itself."

And Martín, chewing his coca as if nothing had happened: "Now, who knows but what maybe that tree did walk off by itself."

Then Pablo lost his head and whipped out his knife and threw himself at Martín. Just one blow in the breast. He didn't even have time to say *"Ay."* Four years now Martín has been dead.

The balsa trees are getting scarcer every day. There are still a few and their owners keep loving watch over them, but they make us wait while they grow. If not for them, how would we cross the Marañón? By joining them together we make our square rafts which cross the river until they rot or are swept away by it. The stories they could tell!

Up the river there is a valley called Shicún where many balsa trees grow. Their owners do a good business building rafts and those who buy them bring them down the river. We men from Calemar have often gone to Shicún, but not all of us have come back.

What a feeble little structure, the raft, poised upon the roaring waters as on danger itself. It carries the life of the man of the Marañón valleys on it, and he stakes it as on the toss of a coin.

2

Old Matías's Story

It was the last days of March and the level of the river was falling. One day we brought a stranger across without much trouble. The young fellow wore boots, a silk handkerchief at his neck, and a broad-brimmed felt hat. The elegance of his attire contrasted sharply with the homely garments we use in the valley: straw hat, homespun cotton shirt, coarse flannel pants, heavy shoes or flapping sandals, and sometimes a big red bandanna around our neck to protect it from the mustard plaster of the sun. He was riding a big, fine sorrel, but it was strange to our part of the country and we had to tow it behind a raft by a rope. The saddle outfit was bright with silver trimming, like the rider's spurs and revolver, which he wore in a holster hung from his belt.

The gentleman was white, tall, and his glance was keen and sparkling. He was as thin as a reed and looked as though he might suddenly snap at the waist. His soft clear voice was accompanied by polite gestures of the hands. One had only to look at him to see that he was not from that part of the country where the men are squat like rocks and talk in a high thundering voice suited to the broad open spaces or to dialogue with crags.

The stranger was staying at the house of old Matías, the largest in all the valley, and was putting up his mosquito netting on the porch. The old man watched

him as he put the white canopy into place, and finally
he asked him: "What might your name be and what
have you come to do here?"

The young man answered politely enough, although
an ironic smile showed at the corners of his thin lips:
"Osvaldo Martínez de Calderón, at your orders, and
I have come to study this part of the country."

Then he went on to explain that he came from Lima,
that he was an engineer, who his parents were, and that
he was trying to organize a company to develop the natural resources of the region. The old man scratched the
back of his head, pushing his straw hat down over one
eye, pursed his mouth, squinted up his eyes. It was evident that he wanted to make a joke or an objection of
some sort, but all he said was: "You are welcome in
this house, young man, and I wish you good luck!"

Don Matías Romero lives with his wife, Doña Melcha, who is as old as he, and their son Rogelio. Arturo
Romero lives in a house a little way off, for he has been
married for some time. The old man's house has two
rooms and a porch, like the good house it is. The wind
rustles through the thatch of the roof, and fans its
wings against the reed walls of the house, bringing relief
from the never-ending sultriness of these valleys.

That afternoon I went to the old man's house to see
the newcomer and to chat a while. At the end of the
porch Rogelio was stretched out in his bunk while the
stranger, Don Matías and Arturo were sitting on homemade cedar stools beside the door.

"Come in, man . . . come in," the friendly voice of
the old man called out.

There were many wrinkles woven into his and Doña
Melcha's dark faces, but their hearts were stout. Gray-
ing chin whiskers, like a goat's, gave the old man a
roguish look. Arturo was a grown man, as the black
bristles which stood out over his upper lip bore witness.
Roge's face was covered with fuzz like a green peach;
here and there a whisker stood out like a maguey on the
plain.

A stranger from so far away—where in the devil is

that Lima they talk so much about?—is a novelty, and we started to talk about many things. The afternoon was coming to a close and the heat was damp and oppressive. A smell of plowed earth floated in the air and the crickets and locusts sang. From an orange tree golden balls dropped softly and in the top of an *arabisco* a shimmering blue flock of turtle-doves cooed. Old Melcha stood cooking over the fireplace built at the foot of a mango tree that grows beside the door and the smell which reached us was a promise of the good treatment the guest was to receive. We chewed coca and smoked the fine cigarettes which the newcomer gave us. He answered our questions quickly and, on the other hand, seemed astonished at everything he saw. We had to explain even what our lime gourds were, and that we used them to carry lime to chew with our coca, and he carefully examined mine which had a carved horn rim and a cover of the same with a little grinning monkey squatting on it. He took off the cover and when he tried the point of the wire on the back of his it stuck him. We laughed and he turned the color of a red pepper.

There was no letup in the stranger's questions and Don Matías gave his tongue free rein. The old man was one of those who never got tired of talking about his own region.

"What was the flood like, sir? First thing it carried away half a yucca field and two rafts which were down below, where we build them, pulled up at a place where the water had never reached since the times old Julián, God rest his soul, used to tell about."

"It was bad, wasn't it?" asked the stranger.

"There hasn't been anything like it in years, sir. Don Julián has been dead these ten years," he added.

"Yes, indeed." And he went on: "The only raft left was Rogelio's, his"—and he pointed to his son who went on chewing his coca—"and the boy had built it without half trying, out of poor poles he had got down over the cliffs on the other side. It is so little, as you've probably seen, that it looks like a handful of brush floating

around on the water The worst of it was that people
came down and stopped along the other shore after
walking so many miles in the hope of getting across.
The most plaguesome of all were the ones from Celendín. Those buggers! To sell the hats they make those ras-
cals go around everywhere even in the worst of the
rainy season. There were cattle dealers, also, and important people, and sometimes Indians, too. They all
waited there for us to ferry them across. What people!
At night they would light the fires to cook their food at
the foot of some cliff that sloped back like a cave. And
all day long they would be shouting: 'Come take us
across . . . take us across.' And the river roaring and
foaming and rising like it was bewitched."

"A lot of water, eh?" the stranger inquired again.

"A plague of it, sir. It flooded everything. When you
came across you saw those rocks with a black crust on
top all cracked with the sun? Well, those were all covered by the water which left that deposit on them. And
the folks on the other side shouting their heads off, the
way I told you: 'Booatmeen . . . come over, booatmeen.'
And, of course, what the devil, we are boatmen and we
have to bring the people across even though they only
pay eighty centavos apiece. So we started out on Roge's
little raft, using two paddles on each side, rowing as
hard as we could. We set out way up the river so as to
come out at the foot of La Repisa, that flat stone that
sticks way out now, where we used to tie our boats up.
We got there, wet with sweat, and yelled to them to
catch the rope we were going to throw them. Everybody
wanted to get on, but when the water came up to our
ankles we said that was all and we'd have to make another trip for the rest. The peddlers tied their packs on
their backs to keep their wares dry. We were going to
come out way below because of the devilish current that
did as it pleased with the paddles."

"It was like sticking them into thick mud," observed
Arturo, breaking the silence of his coca chewing.

"Afterwards," went on Don Matías, "they had to pull

the raft upstream with a rope from the bank so we could get across."

"What about the animals?" asked the stranger from the coast, probably thinking about his pampered horse.

"They swam across, sir. Though the green ones had to be tied to an experienced one who knew how. There are some that are so wise that they take to the water as soon as their rider dismounts. That's what Don Soria's mule did. He jumped in, saddle, saddlebags, and all. The saddlebag was full of money and Don Soria thought it was going to fall off. It was a sight to see that Christian jumping up and down on the other bank yelling: 'My money . . . my money is going to get lost on that mule.' The only answer he got was the echo from the cliffs, for what could we do, but the mule got over with everything. When Don Soria got across he couldn't believe that everything was safe, except that the saddlebags and saddle were dripping wet. He took out his bills and spread them to dry in the sun, fanning them with his hat and every now and then one blew away, and him running after it. . . ."

Our laughter was like boulders rolling down the slope of mockery. The stranger good-naturedly got a bottle of fine liquor out of his saddlebag and invited us to have a drink. Then he expressed due amazement.

"This is quite a river."

And Don Matías, whose tongue had taken the bit between its teeth, went on: "Oh, sir. Once we saw a jam coming but we rowed with all our might and it just barely missed us. There was a woman aboard who was well along and she turned as white as paper and the minute we got ashore she had a miscarriage. What a flood that was! It won't be forgotten for a long time."

"But you folks could always get across?" the interlocutor went on.

"Don't you believe it, sir. There wasn't a single good raft, and the water was a wild thing. Once—I hate to even think about it—it swelled up like Colluash was in it, that monster almost nobody has seen, but that's like a wolf with a hundred paws and that appears only when the river has to swallow somebody to feed the devil. There were a lot of jams coming down, too, and over on the other side came some fine-dressed gentlemen with white hats and boots and colored handkerchiefs around their necks. They unsaddled their mounts, which swam across as fast as dogs, but nobody went over for fear of Colluash who was surely sniffing around to see how he could get hold of some Christian to eat. There they were on La Repisa, building their fire at night. When it rained or there was a high wind, they didn't even have that. They spent the livelong day digging around the foot of the *pate* trees."

"Around the foot of the *pate* trees?" asked the astonished stranger.

"Yes, sir. That's a funny little tree, that is. From the bark come fibers to make rope, sometimes yellow, sometimes red, depending on the tree. And on the roots there are growths like potatoes or even bigger. These growths fill up with water in the rainy season and that does the tree over the summer, for it lives right among the rocks. The gentlemen dug these growths out to suck the water from them."

"And do you drink the river water here when it's all muddy?"

"No indeed, sir. We collect our water from the ravine which we clean out in the dry season and we store it for the rainy season. Finally the gentlemen's food gave out, too. After about a week one of them climbed up on a rock and shouted: 'Bring us food. We'll pay you.' 'Oood . . . yooou,' answered the cliffs. And the gentleman waved bills around like they were handkerchiefs. We gathered by the bank chewing our coca, about twenty of us. We looked up and down the river that was cursing like a lost soul and nobody felt like trying it. Dolores said that the night before she had heard Colluash roaring. My boys and I would have crossed but the little raft wasn't good enough for the work. And the gentleman climbed up and began shouting still louder: 'Fooood . . . We'll pay you.' And the cliffs answering him as he waved the bills in the air. Finally after watch-

ing them and listening to them so long Rogelio wanted
to go. His mamma and all of us begged him not to, but
he said he'd swim across by himself."

"Who is Rogelio?" inquired the guest.

"That one, over there, my boy Roge," said the old
man, pointing to his son with an air of annoyance because the stranger had not noticed him before. And he
went on pompously, rattling his lime gourd against the
curved knuckle of his left index finger:

"Roge made up a bundle of cooked yuccas and plan-
tains and tied it to his naked back, for he had taken off
his shirt. Then he fastened his pants with many turns of
his broadest band and waded into the river. He usually
dived from a rock into the deep part of the river, but this
time he had the bundle on his back so he went in from
the bank. When he couldn't touch bottom any more he
began to swim. You should have seen the little fellow
raising the foam as he swam. The gentlemen on the
other side yelled to him: 'Come on, boy, come on.' And
we yelled, too: 'Go on, go on.' And his mamma, too.
'Go on, Rogito, go on, son, remember you have to
come back.' And the river roaring and the bundle only
a little spot in the middle of the waves of black water.
But my boy Roge swam hard—who couldn't when he
was twenty!—and he came out right at the foot of La
Repisa. The gentlemen threw him a rope and he climbed
right out. It was easier coming back without that bundle
on his back, but even so he came out way down below.
He came toward us walking along the stones of the
bank and he was panting and his breast was all bloody
from a scratch he must have got from a log under the
water. Some said that Colluash had got his claws into
him. Half-scared, half-laughing, my Roge pulled three
red bills out of his mouth, worth a pound each. The
river went down in about three days and we could row
out to the gentlemen."

Don Matías paused while Roge turned over in his
bunk, laughing wholeheartedly now, without the coun-
terweight of his fright. Old Melcha brought in a flat
earthen dish full of burning dung so the smoke would

drive away the mosquitoes. All of us except the rather supercilious stranger were chewing big wads of coca and talking noisily. He did not want to tell us about Lima, but instead he gave us the last of his fine liquor which, when mixed with our rum, makes us lose all our restraint. The white grains of laughter popped gaily in our mouths while the heat of the valley wrapped its warm blanket of purple twilight about us. We ate heartily of the fried chicken with yuccas and sweet potatoes Doña Melcha served us, and bananas which the old man pulled off the bunches we had watched turning yellow all afternoon through the reed wattles of the walls.

It grew dark and Roge lighted a slender wand on which were threaded fruits of the *higuerilla,* peeled and white, which burn with a sputtering flame. The owls and the *pacapacas* made the leaves tremble with their doleful calls. Overhead, the clear sky was aglitter with thousands of stars. It looked like a bowl of burnished bronze. Swarms of mosquitoes began to whine and Don Osvaldo got under his netting.

Arturo, looking up at the bright unclouded sky, spoke: "Here it is summer and we need a raft."

"That's true," answered Rogelio. "There are hardly any trees around here and we'll have to go to Shicún."

They ruminated the idea along with their coca, and for a while none of us said anything. A new raft was needed and must be bought. It would cost about thirty *soles,* but that did not matter. Arturo turned around on his stool.

"You come with us," he said looking at me.

I would have liked to go just to take a few swings with the paddle and drink the rum they make in Shicún where they have cane, a grinding mill and a still. But I remembered that bananas had to be cut and that the new fields needed a mulch of ashes and I would have to burn brush.

"I wish I could, but I can't. I've got to plant that land that I cleared and I'm going to burn brush. If I don't hurry, the grass will get ahead of me."

Arturo rattled his gourd and turned toward his

brother: "How about you, man? Is the great swimmer coming?"

Rogelio was strutting like a rooster those days, courting Florinda, but he didn't need to be coaxed to make the trip. He did put on a few airs, but he answered: "Suits me. But first we'll have something to drink at the hacienda and we'll bring back a few gourdfuls of liquor from there to set up drinks for everybody. This money is burning a hole in my pocket."

Doña Melcha was informed that she would have to prepare food for them, and old Matías went rambling on about whatever came into his head. The engineer, drugged with the heat, was snoring under his netting. The old man was planning to wash gold at the Recodo del Lobo to sell to the traders during the fair at Pataz. I was cheerful, thinking of my banana field, and his gold did not interest me very much. I planned to go to the fair too, but I had enough with the stuff from out of my garden: coca and perhaps bananas. Arturo and Roge said they would decide what they were going to do when they got back. Perhaps they would take something to sell or, most probably, they would do the ferrying. They would see about that later but, anyway, they would have money to celebrate with.

The bats were flying about tracing swift flourishes in the darkness.

The next day, very early in the morning, the stranger saddled his horse and set out on the narrow road that zigzagged up the slope. The brothers left, shouldering their knapsacks and ponchos, following a barely visible path that skirts the riverbank to Shicún, turning and twisting endlessly over the rocks along the shore or climbing up the slopes when the river cuts under the cliffs. They were putting up the money for the raft between the two of them.

3

Lucindas and Florindas

Nestling under the trees, not far from the house of old Matías, was the house of Arturo. It, and the other cabins, awoke amidst a concert by *chiroques* and *chiscos* to which the *jergones* add their strident note. They were lulled to sleep at night by the sound of the owls and *pacapacas,* and all day they heard the melodious notes of the *pugos* and the turtle-doves. There was always the sound of the birds in the trees, and the Marañón, with its bass major, accompanied the neverceasing song.

It was Lucinda who was rattling the cooking gourds about inside. Lucinda was from the town. In her green eyes there was rain with sunshine and she was all grace as she walked, her pliant body swaying like a papaya tree. From her womb she had borne a son named Adán. The child stayed close to his mother's skirts and would not wander away because she filled him with a fear of snakes. So it was a great delight for the boy when Arturo, at home among his plantings, mattock in hand, grubbing the wiry grass out of the coca and peppers, suddenly called out: "The shotgun."

Then Adán, who could barely balance himself, went wobbling toward his father with the gun in his arms, looking askance at this strange object which gleamed like the gold in gentlemen's teeth. While the *pugos*

courted musically in the treetops, Arturo carefully
pulled back the hammer so the tight springs would make
no noise and then a violent crack shattered the harmonious rhythm of the valley. The shot reverberated
among the crags.

In a swirl of feathers the doves fell fluttering to the
ground and Adán ran over and wrung their necks. He
noticed that, just as they died, a blue fly escaped from
under their wings. His father explained to him that all
the *pugos* carry one of these under their wings to warn
them of danger. If the fly gets careless the hunter can
come on them by surprise and shoot them. That's why
people say to a person who gets careless about things:
"Man, your fly's asleep."

The child went back dragging the gun behind him
and squeezing the warm bodies of the birds in his
bloodstained little hands. It was a delight like no other
to feel himself weighed down by the still-smoking gun
and the birds dripping blood, and, all around, the vast
forest full of snakes and dangers.

As Adán grew, so did his ambitions. He dreamed
of the day when he could handle a paddle and raise
the water the way his father did; but for the moment
his dream was to climb the alligator pear tree where
the *jergones* had built a marvellous nest of weeds, fibers
and moss in which a whole family of them lived. His
mother told him that he would have to put off these
ambitions until he was bigger and he had to accept her
advice since his little hands could barely scratch the
bark of the tree.

The love of his parents, which sank into his soul
like the roots of a tree into the ground, consoled him.
Arturo had waited a long time for him and so had
his mother. He was really the link between them, for
what good is a sterile woman? She is complete only
if she has children. Then she is water for thirst,
bread for hunger, and, besides, a furrow—a furrow
for life.

Arturo and Lucinda knew one another in Sartín.
While he is on his way to Shicún for the raft it might

be a good thing to learn their story which, in great part, has to do with the river. A river of water and a river of blood, both turbulent and convulsed, both ready to seize upon a human being and tear him to pieces like a poor branch.

Five or six years ago—six it was because our Marañón has flooded six times since then—the two brothers went to a festival in Sartín.

When they arrived it was already dark. The beat of the drums and the wailing of the flutes received them as they trotted up the slope. As they came in they could hear the strumming of guitars and voices singing suggestive *marineras:*

> "As you went up the stairs
> I saw your blue stockings."

The light of kerosene lamps or flickering candles came through the doors cutting yellow patches in the darkness of the streets. There the shadows held their dance. Groups of drunken Indians wandering about, talking incoherently or breaking into mournful song, scrambled out of the way of the dashing horsemen who were heralded by the clatter of hoofbeats. Some of them shouted: "Hooray for the bosses" and the Romeros rode like a whirlwind through the streets to pull up short in front of a house where a bass drum proclaimed its full-throated presence. The horses snorted and twitched their ears nervously refusing to advance, but spurs dug into their flanks and they lunged forward madly riding down the Indians. Arturo and Roge reached their inn shouting out the name of its mistress.

Doña Dorotea received them kindly, with the affable manners of the townsfolk, serving them glasses of *chicha* that had been prepared for the festival and which they drank off in long swallows while, beside them, the horses nickered sniffing the near-by alfalfa fields.

"How's everything in the valley?"

"It's still there."

The half-breeds gaily unsaddled their sweaty horses. To the little table on the porch came Lucinda carrying dishes of fragrant food. The tallow candle threw enough light to reveal the girl, as she came back and forth, taking good care of the strangers' wants.

Arturo, as he gnawed at a guinea-pig leg, nudged Roge: "Pretty nice, eh?"

Indeed she was nice. In the two years they had missed coming to the festival she had ripened like a fruit. When she came near the table Arturo looked her over to his full satisfaction. The wan light enveloped her, bringing out her finely modeled face and pointed breasts. Her green eyes danced gaily under the firm arch of her brows. Gossip had it that she was the daughter of an English miner who stopped one night at Doña Dorotea's house. It was probably true because the lady was known to have a "roving eye," and the girl never called Don Antuco, Doña Dorotea's late husband, father.

She stood in the door, watching them start off to a dance after finishing their hearty feast, which had been washed down with numerous drinks. After taking a few steps Arturo turned back.

"Aren't you going?"

"My mamma doesn't want me to."

"Bah. I'm going to talk to her."

Doña Dorotea finally gave in, urging them to go to the house of her friend Pule, and not to stay too late. Pleased and excited, they agreed to everything and started off. Lucinda walked, scattering words right and left as she went. Holding tightly to her skirt, like an infantile watchman, walked her little brother, by order of her mother. The Indians, shadows in the night, crowded the streets blocking their way and Arturo pushed them aside with his hands, saying:

"Make way for beauty."

There was a smell of food strong with chile and pepper, of corn liquor and damp wool, and very close,

beside Arturo arising from Lucinda's fluttering breasts,
the fragrance of Florida water and young flesh. He bit
his lips and his nostrils dilated with his deep breath.
As they crossed a ditch he took her arm and a sensation
of gentle warmth remained in his hand.

"What a pretty girl you've become."

And with a gleam of her firm white little teeth she
answered: "And what a liar you've become."

A Roman candle shot up a shower of light and ex-
ploded in the air shaking the dark curtains the night
had dropped over the vigil of the gay little town. High
up, far away, tiny red lights flickered. They were the
fires of the huts that clung to the slopes of the hills and
which, in wait for the return of the merrymakers, had
not yet gone to sleep.

Lucinda was the belle of the dance at Doña Pule's,
whirling like a spindle to the rhythmic sound of the
dance, her full-lipped mouth and sparkling green eyes
always smiling. The musicians were two Indians, with
their drums and flutes, and a lame man who played the
accordion and sang. The Indians, with their plangent
flutes and their tense drums, which were the echo of
distant peals of thunder, poured into the room the
cashuas of the highlands. When they got tired, the
accordion player introduced the *chiquitas* of the town.
The bellows writhed in and out, over the player's cush-
ioned wrist, panting a twanging accompaniment to the
song which made the lank, half-breed mustaches quiv-
er and the dancers whirl about:

"Since Junín and Ayacucho, liberty . . .
My dark one, long live Peru, my beauty, long live
     Peru.
When will my Junín come to end your proud
     tyranny,
My dark one, long live Peru, my beauty, long live
     Peru."

Lucinda had turned as sweet as molasses. Arturo
danced madly in front of her, but the girl always

outdid him with her riotous display of steps. The
furious stamping of the *cholos'* heavy shoes raised
the dust. The couples were tireless. Roge who had
found himself a partner to stay in the dance winked
an eye at his brother.

"Man, when you're older and more important, you
have all the luck."

There were buckets, jugs, glasses, gourds of *chicha*
everywhere. Arturo left the room and came back clasping bottles of rum against his broad chest.

"Look, there's nothing small about these valley
fellows."

It was a deluge of happiness. The air reeked with
alcohol, strong enough to make you drunk just smelling
it. Lucinda felt a queer tingling in her veins and she
shivered all over when Arturo, taking his red bandanna
in both hands, put it behind her neck and drew her still
closer to him until her breasts, tense with dancing and
desire, brushed against his thick chest. What a man,
this fellow from the valley! The little brother was asleep
in a corner, and it filled her with happiness to feel that
her eyes were talking to this man as they had never
dared do before and that her hands were about his
strong and flexible waist. Their feet began to move
softly, weaving a counterpoint of surrender and flight,
of return and triumph.

Doña Pule had served the customary chicken broth,
and the hour of leave-taking had come. Down the
streets they stumbled over the Indians who had
stretched out to sleep their heavy drunken slumber.
Sharp gusts of icy air blew through the late night, and
in a moment dawn would arrive to embrace the village
with the long kiss of its light.

Arturo was holding Lucinda by the arm. His heavy
hand held her tight, but the girl knew that it was another
pressure, not that of his hand, but stronger, that kept
her beside him. Her blood had cooled, but in her breast
there was a new feeling, as deep as the night and as
bright as the day that is about to break. She felt like the
night waiting for the day. "Can this be love?" she

wondered, and a shiver went through her. Arturo did
not feel it for he was walking beside her, enjoying as
never before a familiar song:

"If my dark girl would only
Cross the river with me,
I would pay her passage
And carry her all the way."

It was a song that Lucinda had heard many times, too,
but now she found in it a new charm and it seemed
to presage a trip and a new life. With Arturo
perhaps? They walked very close and they felt themselves bound together although they did not know that
it was love that had come, because the feeling that
stirred in their hearts had become a song and a call to
adventure. But the words Roge spoke to the sleepy little fellow behind them sounded as though they came
from some faraway place.

In the house Lucinda could hear the brothers through
the reed and mud walls spreading their bed with the
saddle pads of their horses and covering themselves
with the blankets her mother had left in the little room.
They talked on and on about one thing and another
and finally they grew still.

She slipped down beside her little brother who was
already asleep. She put her arms around him and kissed
him with unwonted tenderness, and clasped herself
against him full length. Close, close beside him, as
though he were Arturo.

A rooster flapped its wings and crowed in the
distance.

They awoke when the sun, high in the sky, was
burnishing the village with gold. The crowds were
having difficulty moving through the narrow streets
and they milled about in the square where the bands
of dancers were performing. There were the Indian
women in their red, green and yellow skirts, their

garishness subdued a little by the drab yellow of the men's ponchos; the gentlemen with their starched linen suits which crackled as they walked; the men from Celendín with their striped linen ponchos standing beside their piles of percale, hats and gew-gaws; the white homemade felt hats of the Indians of Pataz and the red pottery cooking dishes of the people from Mollepata, all in a framework of white-walled houses with red roofs that surrounded the square. From the porches of these houses the local magnates—in high boots, riding breeches, hats pushed back on their necks—watched the festival, drinking and firing their revolvers into the air. Their wives were wearing new dresses and heavy fringed shawls over their shoulders for the occasion.

The square was a basket of bright beads under a hollow blue mirror along which a gleaming disk advanced, pouring out its golden hues.

Lucinda went to the festival with the boys from the valley. She had put on all her best clothes and looked as if she had just stepped out of a bandbox. A blue Spanish shawl, white blouse and green skirt. On her head a hat of white straw, and high-heeled shoes on her little feet. The boys had brought their finery out of the saddlebags to keep pace with her. They were wearing new palm-leaf hats, white shirts, gray and black striped cassimere pants and heavy shoes. At their throats red bandannas. Arturo—the *cholo* was vain and liked to swagger a little—wore a band of the Peruvian national colors around his hat. They made up a chattering trio as they stood in a corner beside the women who sold *chicha* and food, sitting beside their tall pots and surrounded by gourds cut in half and filled with potatoes colored with red pepper and fried guinea pig.

They talked as they ate and drank slowly from the gourds.

"The festival is better than ever," said Arturo.

"I hope it stays this way till the end. No matter what happens, remember that I am your brother," answered Roge.

Lucinda said nervously: "Good Heavens . . . what are these people thinking about. . . . Of course, the festival is going to be all right."

And then turning to the wrinkled old woman who sat hidden behind the pile of gourds: "Lady, this guinea pig must have been a granddaddy. . . . let's have a little drink to make it set better."

The bands of dancers sang and danced untiringly, hemmed in by circles of spectators. They wore costumes of variegated colors and strings of glass and pearl beads. Fastened to their full breasts and on their sleeves were little mirrors which danced and glittered, reflecting the radiance of the sun in all directions.

The group of the *coriquingas* told the story of this beautiful bird of the highlands. One of the members, dressed in black and white to imitate the colors of the bird, described its lonely life and praised its beauty.

"I am a pretty girl, I am a *coriquinga,*
Because I am so pretty they call me the gringa."

The chorus answered, agreeing at times and at others answering ironically, which aroused the ready, noisy laughter of the bystanders.

The group of the fox and the sheep mimicked the attacks on the flock. That of the condor lavished praise on the king of the heights. The very famous one of the "lazybones" is an ironical comment on human and family relations. The "lazybones" sang in a deep voice:

"My saddle and my wife,
I lost them both sometime back.
Devil fly away with the wife,
It's the saddle I want back."

"That's certainly the truth," observed a *cholo.*

"No wonder, anybody would miss a saddle," pointed out the wrangler from the Pomabamba ranch who was standing by. His poncho was tossed over one shoulder, and he was barely able to keep on his feet.

The women of the chorus answered in high-pitched voices that the lazybones was a worthless good-for-nothing who never did a day's work and that his wife left him because she was tired of working from sunup to sundown to support him. But lazybones was not so easily bested, and he changed his theme but kept the irony:

> "I'm looking for my wife,
> A good-looking girl with tousled hair.
> If she happens to be prettied up
> There's a nigger in the woodpile somewhere."

The girls in the circle of spectators—dressed for the holiday in clean dresses and with their hair smoothly braided—blushed at the guffaws of the men whose breath reeked of coca and alcohol as they shouted their approval. After each verse the bands of dancers wove and danced in and out in time to the music of drums, harps or violins, and then began another verse of the song from the scene they represented. At times they went over to the houses and recited verses in praise of the ranchers and their wives. These, models of largesse, answered with a generous gift of small change.

There were more and more groups of dancers. They went through the village, up and down every path, followed by their *mestros,* the Indian or half-breed musicians. The homemade violins sounded as though they had a buzzfly shut up in their bellies; the harps vibrated with difficulty against their rough conical sounding boards, and only the drums and flutes preserved the purity of their deep and sweet voices.

The bands of "Moors and Turks" arrived, those devils who carried great knives to kill all Christians who feared God, and others, who were just singers, praising the ranchers and the Church:

> "This road leads, leads to a Holy House,
> Leads to a Holy House, that of the Blessed Trinity."

When the band of the *oroyeros* appeared there was great enthusiasm, especially in the men from the valley and Lucinda. The band represented the crossing of the Marañón on ropes and they came up shouting while a noisy crowd formed around them.

"Let's get out of here," said Arturo, elbowing his way through the crowd, followed by Lucinda and Roge. "This is like a whirlpool in the river."

A group of girls wearing flowing blue dresses and wreaths of flowers in their hair sang songs alluding to the river. The two men in the group, with a grave air, brandished the machetes they carried at their belts in leather sheaths pretending to cut down the trees, which were already at hand and which they were going to use. Somebody handed them shovels and they dug holes into which they set the tree trunks and then swung two thick parallel leather ropes between them. The river was supposed to run below. The songs were full of the roaring waters. The waters wanted men to devour. The river was greedy and fierce. Then the men started across, walking on one rope and holding on by the other. It was a difficult business. "Courage, brother, courage, there below lies the Marañón," said the song. The men, making the ropes tremble, paused. The danger made them dizzy. They hesitated. They felt faint. Perhaps they were going to fall. Yes, fall and be lost amidst the raging waters. "Courage, brother, courage, there below lies the Marañón." Perhaps they would die. The ropes were shaking harder than ever and they could scarcely hold on. "There below lies the Marañón." But they were going on. They were more than halfway across. "Courage, brother, courage." They had recovered their balance and two long steps brought them to the other side and they broke into loud shouts of triumph. Then the violin poured out even more piercing wails and the harp twanged with all its might and the drums and flutes broke wildly into the notes of a dance. The members of the band formed a circle around the *oroyeros* who went through their dance. Overhead the sun, too, was very happy. The blue sky was aglow.

The band sung of how daring was the river, but the men were more daring still.

Ever-present in the distance, the spectators could hear the murmur of the river. Arturo and Roge remembered their boundless river, so huge that there was no way of measuring it, and a surge of pride went through them as they told themselves that it was not on tight-stretched ropes overhead that they challenged it but on nimble rafts launched on its current that they subdued it day after day. Lucinda looked at Arturo, and something like a river ran from her vitals to her throat, savage and beautiful in its power.

"It must be beautiful," she said.

"It is, certainly it is. If you want to, let's go. The ropes are all right for the fellows from the highlands. I cross it on a raft. Come on, girl."

How beautiful to cross the river and live beside the river with this man who was its master. It was probably blue like the pool of the mountain stream that ran close to the village, and perhaps black in winter, but anyway very big, "so big that nobody knows where it ends," as the songs said, and "with a terrifying voice." But Arturo and Roge were not afraid of it so she was not either. It must be a different sort of world and a different sort of life.

"All right, let's go."

They exchanged handkerchiefs. Arturo's throat disappeared from sight under a bright blue scarf while the girl's wrist was shackled by the vivid red one worn by the man from the valley. The colors were as intense as their emotions. Her eyes were a glossy sea green and his, the obscure brown of the river. Scarfs and eyes and color. For the time being the festival did not exist for them. There were only scarfs and eyes and colors.

Then, caught up by the multitude once more, the couple advanced, aware again of the groups of dancers and all there was to be seen. In the two large houses that fronted the square there was dancing, for there had been two weddings in the families of the ranchers at mass that morning and they were celebrating them. The

Indians gathered around the door and the owners appeared from time to time to throw them handfuls of coins which produced noisy confusion as they scrambled for the money.

"If they paid that well for work all those Indians would be rolling in money," observed Arturo.

The priest who had come to the festival was in one of the reveling groups and he did not take a back seat for anybody when it came to drinking and dancing. When he appeared at the door he said to the Indians in a voice that seemed to come from far away, far behind the billowing curve of his stomach: "My children, God likes to see his faithful enjoy themselves. If you drink prudently there is no harm in it."

But the two State Troopers—a novelty at the festival—who happened to be passing through the square at that moment with their rifles over their shoulders and sword and revolver in their belts, did not feel the same way about it. They belonged to the new corps that had just been stationed at Huamachuco and they had taken it upon themselves to see that not a living soul was to drink more than he could carry. They began by fining Don Roque, the rancher, who had got so drunk the night before that he could not walk straight, two pounds. He paid the fine and then gave them two pounds more, saying: "This is in advance, for tomorrow I'm going on another one."

Since then they had been snickered at by the townspeople and refused entrance to the gatherings in the houses of the well-to-do, so they had taken their spite out on the half-breeds and Indians. The latter eyed the rifles with respect, and looked upon the felt hats and shining leggings and olive-drab uniforms with their gilt buttons and red stripes with admiration.

As they went about the square they met Arturo and Lucinda. They stopped them both, and after whispering together and looking at Lucinda, one asked Arturo, "Listen, friend, where are you from?"

"From my part of the country, sir."

The other guard drew his brows down over his

furious eyes, and put his hand on the butt of his
revolver.

"You insolent fellow! We know you're from your part
of the country but we want to know what your name
is. We'll teach you respect for the State Troopers. . . ."

"I'm from the valley, sir, from Calemar."

Lucinda's eyes were more beautiful than ever as
they pleaded mutely, but her lips were closed by a vague
fear. What these men wanted was for her to ask them
for something and then they would give in and strike up
a friendship. . . .

Arturo added: "I've never been in trouble, gentlemen."

The two asked sarcastically: "Where's your army
registration book? Let's see it. These people never do
their duty by their country."

It was not conscription time, but this was the best
way to catch a country fellow. They kept smiling un-
pleasantly until Arturo dug it out of the bottom of one
of his pockets.

"Here it is, sir. I've always gone to town and registered."

He handed over a dirty little yellowed dog-eared
document. One of the guards examined it and wrote
down the name in his notebook while he recovered his
dignity, and said solemnly as he handed it back: "You
may go on."

Arturo and Lucinda walked through the group
that had gathered to see a possible arrest. He was
indignant and said to her: "It was you they wanted.
. . . They're all a bunch of dirty dogs. . . . The old-
time ones were better."

Twilight was descending slowly. The hills—red, violet, yellow—had dressed themselves like the bands of
dancers for their vespertine dance about the town
that had fallen silent with sorrow at seeing the last
day of the festival come to a close. People began to
go to their lodgings or take the roads that would lead
them back to their huts. An occasional Indian musician
who had had more than was good for him went blow-

ing his flute and pounding his drum along the precip-
itous paths. Boom-boom . . . boom . . . boom. The flute
faded plaintively away letting out an occasional howl.
Boom . . . boom . . . boom . . . boom.

The night flapped its condor wings.

Roge returned to their inn somewhat befuddled
with all the drinks he had taken with the valley people
he had met. Arturo told him what had happened with
the troopers and the two talked the matter over lazily.

"Too bad you didn't bring along the old persuader."

"How was I to know those two bastards were going to be here?"

"It's always a good idea. Guns were made to be
carried."

They were referring to a rusty revolver that hung in
a saddlebag in Arturo's cabin. They were sitting on the
porch and the troopers who were walking past the
house threw them an inquisitive glance. The brothers
restrained the curses they would have uttered as Doña
Dorotea came out to talk with them. They told her
they did not bring any coca because they had sold it all
before, that there was always lots of fruit and that the
river . . . well . . . the river kept right on rolling along.
. . . The mistress of the inn laughed, and as they offered
to bring her whatever she wanted the next year, she told
them that she especially wanted *annatto* and *cañafistola*.
She held forth for an hour about how good they were
for this ailment or that ailment and, as a matter of
fact, for all the ills that flesh is heir to. That evening
they went to Doña Rosario's. Lucinda did not want
to refuse, nor Doña Dorotea either, although the little
brother had to stay home because he was sleeping like
a log.

Arturo coaxed ingratiatingly: "It's the last day of
the festival, the very last day," and both the women
consented.

Doña Rosario, a very pious person, had erected in
the best room of her house an altar to the Patroness of
Sartín. The Virgin stood in a corner behind a row of
candles, surrounded by flowers and rosy pasteboard

cherubs. Two harps and a violin provided music and one of the harpists sang in a cracked voice. Whenever a dancer turned his back on the Virgin he always asked her forgiveness before he did so. Enthusiasm mounted as the *chicha* and rum took effect, and the room became filled with dancers. Along the walls, on boxes and dilapidated chairs, only wrinkled toothless old men and women were left. They laughed and talked in quavering voices as they smacked their lips over the sweetened corn porridge and the drinks. The dancers wove in and out and put their arms around one another. The apologies to the Virgin grew fewer and fewer. The dancers clasped one another, bumped together, moved away and came together again with a rhythmic movement of hips and ankles. Arturo and Lucinda, in a corner outside the vortex, were dancing close together, longing to be ever closer, their drink-heavy breath intermingling.

"So we're going to Calemar?"

"Oh, yes, but my mamma is going to want us to get married."

"That's all right. The priest is still here. Tomorrow we'll get married."

Arturo, whose happiness knew no bounds, shouted out the revelry cry: "Bring on the *chicha* and the brandy, people here are thirsty." Lucinda ran and came back with a full glass and the two drank from it, each putting his lips where the other's had been. At this point Roge interrupted them.

"Brother, it looks like there'll be three of us going back."

Arturo's reply was cut short, for just then the troopers came in with their rifles across their shoulders, looking over the gathering with a scornful, high-and-mighty air. The couples went on dancing, but they felt themselves under scrutiny and it dampened their pleasure. "Spoilsports, that's what they are," complained a woman's voice.

One of the troopers walked over to Arturo.

"Lend me your partner."

And without waiting for an answer he began dancing

with Lucinda, but he was so awkward that everybody began to laugh. As for the girl, she barely went through the steps, making it plain that she was only dancing with the man because she could not help herself. The other guard walked up to Arturo.

"You're laughing, are you, you son-of-a-bitch? You'd better watch out."

And he assumed a threatening air, one foot well forward and his hand on his revolver. Arturo stood quietly, thinking that if he did not answer they would leave and everything would go on as before. But the ones who left were the dancers, slipping silently away, as if to hide. Very few remained, and the worst of it was that both of the troopers insisted on dancing with Lucinda. She looked at Arturo across a world of disgust and desolation. The brothers talked together in a corner and then the older one stepped forth resolutely.

"Listen, gentlemen, you were not invited to come here and this girl is going to marry me tomorrow so I would thank you not to bother her any more."

The troopers, as though someone had suddenly touched a spring, drew together shoulder to shoulder and cocked their rifles, making a great show of pulling back the bolts with a noisy clatter. "Bah, that stuff is to scare the Indians," remarked a huge half-breed as he stopped the dance he was going through. The other couples stopped too. Doña Rosario was all terrified eyes. The other half-breeds began to mutter as the *chicha* inside them brought to life their fighting instincts which, as a rule, were quiescent. A hundred eyes glittered like knives as they faced the guards who realized they would have to find some way out of the situation.

"Out of here with these two impudent valley fellows, out with them."

And they unsheathed their sabers, with the idea of using the flat of their swords against them, but it never got beyond the intention. The half-breeds flung themselves savagely upon the troopers and disarmed them. It became a free-for-all, punctuated by the shrill cries of the women. With a hard punch Roge knocked down one of the troopers. Arturo grabbed the other by the neck, and they fell to the ground and rolled about on the floor, clutching, punching and hitting one another. "Give it to him, man ... give it to him," the other half-breeds encouraged Arturo, brandishing their fists. With a blow to the jaw Arturo knocked him senseless. Then resting back on his heels, he lifted him in the air like a rag doll. The trooper's head thudded as it landed against the floor.

The two brothers and Lucinda, followed by the crowd, dashed to the door and disappeared in the darkness. Only the troopers remained in the room, the blood from their noses and mouths staining the floor, stretched out full length before the Virgin who kept her supplicating eyes fixed Heavenward. The guns lay where they had fallen, barely gleaming in the flickering light of the candles. The fixity of their black pupils had disappeared.

Doña Rosario shouted from the doorway, agitating the wild vanes of her arms, "The governor ... get the governor."

But only Indians sidled up to the door, and stopped there, looking fearfully at the rigid figures of the troopers. Their coppery, sharp-profiled faces stood out against the black, sound-filled night. There was a suggestion of a smile on them. "The governor ... get the governor." The voice of a drum bore witness that the governor was busy with other things.

The two valley fellows and Lucinda reached home after a wild dash through the streets, knocking down passers-by and bringing to the doors curious faces which were able to distinguish in the mass of darkness only three fleeing figures. Their conversation was brief:

"We've got to go right away."

"My mamma won't like it."

"Come on, you wait for me at the corner."

Lucinda made a gesture of hesitation. She wanted to go in the house and throw her arms around her mother and never let go of her. But at the same time she felt an inescapable command within her, a powerful voice that came from some far-off world of dreams, the deep voice of another world . . . and she walked swiftly toward it, there where Arturo and a new life were calling her.

Meanwhile Roge went for the horses while his brother got everything ready to saddle quickly. As he adjusted the stirrups Doña Dorotea came out.

"Are you leaving?"

"Yes, we got into a fight with the troopers."

"Well, lads, you had better move fast, for if they catch you they'll have you rotting in jail for God knows how long."

The stiff dry leather needed greasing. It took forever to fasten the buckles.

"Yes, indeed, you're in a nice fix."

At last that was done. Now to fold the sweaty gray woolen saddle pads, which gave off an acrid smell.

"Where's Lucinda?"

"She'll be along soon."

Roge came up with the horses which whinnied eagerly as they realized that they were homeward bound. It was the work of a second to saddle and mount.

"Good-bye, Doña Doro. Good luck, and, God willing, we'll be seeing you next year."

"Thanks for your hospitality."

They dashed off at a gallop, but they pulled up short at the corner. Why? Doña Dorotea peered after them. The horses pranced nervously. Is that a woman that is being lifted up onto one of them? Suddenly it all dawned upon her and she rushed after the group shouting shrilly and desperately: "Lucinda . . . Lucindita."

Her voice was drowned by the fierce gallop of hoofbeats.

It was a long street. Palms, prickly pears, magueys, houses, barking dogs, all were swiftly left behind, wrapped in darkness. Arturo carried his girl before him in the saddle, and her heart beat to the horse's gallop. As they reached the hill he pulled the horse up short.

The labored breathing of the horses kept time to the painful beating of the girl's heart.

Arturo laughed.

"Did that scare you?" and then to his brother, "Where are the troopers' horses?"

"In that barn lot down there."

"Hurry up, turn them loose."

Roge set his horse down the slope and disappeared in the night. There was the sound of a squeaking gate and then the neighing of galloping horses. He was back in a few moments and they started up the steep slope. The horses climbed stoutly up striking sparks from the stones along the winding road. Here and there were the flimsy huts of the Indians and some of them, sitting at their doors, were playing their rustic flutes. The plangent music followed them tenaciously. Lucinda was overwhelmed with grief thinking of her mother, her brother, and the house where she had spent all her days. In contrast to all this rose the huts of the Indians, who played the mournful pipes. She sobbed at the thought that she could never go back. Now they, her mother and her brother, would be crying too. They would be alone and grieving. Why couldn't she go back? They weren't far away yet. And the pipes went on playing, telling her that she was still near them. The tears rolled down her cheek and fell on Arturo's hands, for he was holding her around the waist.

"Are you crying?"

"My mamma. My little brother."

He answered almost brutally: "There's nothing to do about it . . . It's too late now."

It is the voice of the river, imperious and relentless. That of the pipes is barely audible. Lucinda now heard only that voice and she yielded, without further resistance, to the current.

On the crest of the hill they dismounted to tighten the cinches and look down the road. It unrolled below them, silently. They listened carefully; there was not the faintest sound. Nobody was following them. The town huddled below, its presence revealed by the lights shining in the hollow. A firework castle had been lighted and gleamed brilliantly. The distance gave the explosions a hollow sound.

"So long," said Arturo.

They rode gaily down the hillside. Then they began the descent to the Marañón. Even the horses' hoofs clattered merrily. A strange calm had come over Lucinda. She would have liked to talk but she could think of nothing to say and all she did was nestle closer to her man, leaning tightly against him.

The night was dark and the riders let the horses' reins hang slack, for they knew the way better than the men did. It seemed to the girl that the slope must be very steep for every now and then the horses slipped, sending down a shower of pebbles.

"It will be hours before they find their horses."

"Suppose the devils are dead?"

"No danger. Pests like that never die."

"Then let them try to catch up with us."

"You bet."

The brothers laughed as the branches of the trees began to strike them in the face. Arturo said to his girl: "Be careful, bend your head down and shut your eyes."

It must have been a wooded region. The branches tugged at their hats. They heard the sound of water and the unbroken song of crickets and katydids. They were going down . . . going down. The water was nearer now, babbling in a voice that seemed to disappear in a downward direction.

"Is that the Marañón?" Lucinda asked uneasily.

"No, nothing but a brook that runs into it. The river is still far away." The horses splashed through the water, drank a little, and then they rattled over the stones again. But the voice of the water could be heard to one side, along the curves of the road. There were steep steps which the horses took carefully, snuffling, almost smelling at them. With heads hung low they watched the road carefully and descended slowly. Down . . . down . . . At each step Lucinda trembled. Down . . . down . . . down to the hollow of the canyon.

The brook and the road, the men and the beasts were
going down to meet the Marañón, to come together in
it. Hours and hours. To Lucinda the descent was like
a surrender, a voluptuous falling through space.

The men grew silent. The only sound, as they penetrated the darkness, was that of the hoofbeats and the
ripple of running water flowing toward the river. From
time to time a hot hard mouth pressed against Lucinda's neck. She leaned shivering against her man. All
around was the black depth, deep like an abyss,
dizzying. . . .

Now the horses moved silently over soft ground that
seemed damp. The air was filled with the scent of *cheri-
moya* flowers.

"This is the valley the brook goes through."

"Yes, I know."

The horses quickened their pace. Another hour and
they would be at the banks of the Marañón, across from
Shicún. Day was about to break for a faint clarity could
be seen through the leaves and the birds were beginning
to stir in the treetops. The road led to a rise which revealed, surging upward in front of them, a great black
mass against a leaden background. Lucinda's eyes were
wide as she looked on in amazed silence.

"Those are the cliffs," Arturo explained. "That's the
way they look from below at night. We'll be there in a
little while."

The white stretch of road was visible now, and the
horses galloped easily along, around the many curves,
unflagging. Alongside, the *pate* and *arabisco* trees raised
their twisting branches. Suddenly a deep unceasing
sound.

"That's the Marañón."

Lucinda felt as though her ears were filled with foam.
Day was breaking rapidly. A yellow pall hung from the
crest of the hills, but then the light filled the gulch, revealing the purple flowers of the *arabiscos,* the red cliffs,
the yellow dirt along the pebbly road, covered with
whitish dust. Arturo's horse stopped and whinnied.
Roge's did the same. There was the Marañón.

Through the foliage of the trees which balanced themselves on the slope, their branches intertwined as though to support one another, appeared the river in its summer blue. The waters ran along in gentle waves, leaving a white foam along the rocks of the bank. The spurs urged the horses gaily on, and after a half-hour's gallop past shacks and canebrakes, they pulled up on the bank of the river. This side was known as Santa Filomena; the other, as Shicún.

They dismounted and while the brothers loosened the horses' girths Lucinda sat down on a big purplish stone under the shade of a *gualango* tree, and feasted her eyes on the great deep river. Yes, this was the river and these the valleys. Against the sky the red cliffs traced their irregular fretwork, and the sky was blue. The valley of Shicún, in the offing, was a dazzling green. The morning light turned the sand of the two banks into strips of gold and the river appeared again, far up, around a bend, and disappeared, far, far away, behind another, baring the breadth of its rippling blue surface, white along the edges.

The heat made her limbs feel heavy but the languor did not reach her eyes—open wide and bright—where a throbbing, withdrawn soul was in an ecstasy.

The brothers shouted for a raft and began to unsaddle the horses, which then went into the water and easily swam across.

On the opposite bank two men appeared, stepped on a platform of logs, and began to swing broad pieces of wood. Lucinda watched, without asking any questions, for she knew the answers. This was the raft, these were the paddles, and these were the boatmen. Arturo, too, was a boatman. How they bent their backs and knees and dipped the paddles! Now they were near, now they were there. With two powerful strokes they reached the bank and slipped gracefully alongside. They caught hold of a rope Roge threw them and jumped ashore with gay shouts of greeting. They all got aboard the raft, on which they had just loaded the saddles and saddlebags and Arturo, just for the pleasure of it, took one of the paddles. He cleaved the waters, turning them into foam at every stroke, and the boat skimmed quickly ahead through the waves. Lucinda watched him in a maze. This was how she had dreamed of him crossing the river, rowing so strongly. Like this, on the Marañón, the beautiful, the torrential, the powerful. Arturo was like the river or the river like Arturo. Both were strong and for that reason both of them fought.

They had something to eat at the house of Venancio Landauro (one of the men who came over on the raft). This friend served them yucca with chile and dried beef.

"We haven't got any fresh meat. My shotgun is out of order."

"Stay a little while," Landauro invited them cordially.

The brothers laughed but not Lucinda, for she did not hear what they were saying. She was lost in wonder at the garden which stretched before the house, all of it planted in coca which grew under the shiny-fruited alligator pear trees, the thick-foliaged mangos and the orange trees, masses of white flowers whose intense fragrance filled the air.

"You see," Arturo explained, "we're on the run."

He told about his trouble with the troopers and Landauro laughed heartily.

"If they come this way, you be deaf. Even if they shout their heads off, don't you go."

"Don't worry," Landauro reassured him. "I'll be deafer than a post."

They mounted again and started out quickly for Shicún, stopping only to look at the cane mill which Don Augustín, the biggest landowner in the valley, had set up. It was run by a fascinating water wheel which filled and emptied itself and then filled up again, and this made it turn. The mill, too, was very fine with its three iron cylinders that kept turning all the time, shredding to pulp the fields of sugar cane that rippled in the wind like green and yellow lakes.

It was getting dusk when they reached Calemar.

They found the old folks sitting by the fire having their evening meal. At first they were surprised, then overcome with emotion. Old Melcha burst into tears, burying her wrinkled face in Lucinda's full, trembling breast. Now she had a daughter!

Not everything went smoothly, for life is like the river, full of turns and rough crossings. Once two troopers came to arrest the brothers but the minute they entered the valley, from the Shicún side, they were seen. The two men and Lucinda hid in the canebrake and the old folks said they had gone to live in the highlands, over by Bambamarca, or maybe even farther off, who can say. And all through the valley the answer was the same: "They're not here, they left a long time ago."

And even though the acting governor said so, too, the troopers spent three days searching, even in the canebrake. In the end they wanted to set it on fire, but all the people begged them not to, saying that they would have no way to thatch their houses for there was not much good reed to be found. When the garrison at Huamachuco was changed, their fears of the troopers were over. But then Lucinda began to shiver with malaria and old Melcha's herb teas did her no good. Arturo had to go to Huamachuco for quinine. And to make matters worse she had one miscarriage and then another, and the father had to carry two pitiful little bundles to the cemetery. Sorrowfully he dug the graves, bemoaning his misfortune, and he did not even put up a cross. When the feast of the Virgin of Perpetual Help of Calemar came around they got married to make their peace with God. Lucinda quickly recovered and not long afterwards Adán was born. Everybody said it was a miracle the Virgin had performed.

And this was how Lucinda happened to be in Calemar. This was the story. "And what about Florinda?" you will ask. I can only say that the beautiful Lucinda is a fitting match for Florinda and Hormecinda and Orfelinda and Hermelinda, and all the other girls that were born here. One is just as nice as the other. If it came to it, we would all do for them what Arturo did for Lucinda.

Their beautiful names are sweet on our tongues. And they sweeten our lives. They are like the coca. We men of those valleys love them dearly.

4

The Andes, the Jungle, the River

Don Osvaldo Martínez de Calderón climbed the road he had taken, "sometimes on foot and sometimes walking," because his horse, with its broad, heavy hoofs, continually slipped on the sharp edges of the rocks. The good sorrel's sides heaved and he sighed for the broad coastal plains. Don Osvaldo's weariness marched on, weighing him down and counting the curves.

Finally a clump of poplars showed their heads over a rise, and man and beast paused to rest their hearts and take the easy road down. The up-slope had been hard. All along the narrow stretch of road, pebbles and rocks, and, on both sides, cactus and prickly pears with their unsheathed thorns. The *arabiscos,* which need the same warmth as the cane fields, had disappeared and there was now no shade from the trees. The bushes crouched against the ground and seemed animated by a single purpose, to thrust out their claws at passers-by. All the way up the hill the sun had scorched them unmercifully.

Don Osvaldo got back on his horse and in a little while he was under the blessed poplars. He followed the alignment of the trees along the clay road until he made out a red tile roof supported by heavy wooden columns which stood out boldly against white walls.

On the porch with its stone railing there appeared first
an Indian and then an old man with a thick beard.
It was Don Juan Plaza, the rancher of Marcapata. He
wore a yellowish palmleaf hat and was wrapped in a
light brown poncho which left visible only his dull-
finished black boots.

"Get down, sir, get down," called out the old man
as soon as the traveler came near. Don Juan's cordiality toward strangers was as broad and firm as the big
house before which Don Osvaldo dismounted. It gave
him pleasure to see a white face and feel a smooth hand
against his, but his delight was even greater at hearing
clear fluent Spanish, even though it was spoken with
the accent of the region. It was like meeting again the
world he had left behind him, to the south, so far
away. . . .

And his eyes took in the ranch's pleasant surroundings and found delight in its gentle bucolic flavor. To
one side and the other the wheat fields spread their
tender green near the huts of the Indians, in front of
which the magueys lifted up their bare silent slender-
ness. Black-and-white and red heifers nibbled at the
blue thorny fronds of the hedges, and, higher up, along
the gray slope of the hills, the flocks of sheep were
white dots driven along by shrill-barking little dogs.
And up and down the yellowish lanes the Indians an-
ticipated the sunset with the colors of their red skirts
and their multi-hued ponchos.

The old man introduced his family—wife, children
and a swarm of relatives—and they all went into the
dining room, pulling up heavy wooden chairs to a
pleasant table. It was an enormous room whose bare
white walls echoed the words that were spoken. The
young man helped himself to milk and dark bread,
while the old man talked of this and that, and a furry
little dog watched him with a friendly air.

"Believe me when I tell you what a pleasure this
is for me. This is so out of the way that whenever
I meet a civilized person it is like a revelation to me.

Yes, indeed, my dear Don Osvaldo . . . Yes, indeed, sir."

"The same things happen to me, Don Juan. Those half-breeds at Calemar are pleasant enough, but they are interested only in their own affairs. You could never talk to them as man to man; they wouldn't understand what you were saying . . ."

The engineer gave the pup bits of bread soaked in milk, and then he answered the rancher's innumerable questions. What about Lima? And politics? And the government? Is there going to be a revolution? The young man found it hard to answer satisfactorily because he did not know about these matters. He might have been able to give a long talk on Joan Crawford or Clark Gable, but it was apparent that Don Juan was not up on such matters. He talked enthusiastically about the new avenue that had been built and the Parque de la Reserva and finally told him that he had fled from the ease of the capital and had come to this part of the country as a prospector.

"So you're going to explore the region, are you? Then you'll need guides, won't you?" inquired the old man solicitously.

"Yes, I will."

The old man blew a reed whistle and in a little while a young Indian servant came in. He listened with great attention and it seemed as though he were watching rather than listening to the words. He wore only a shirt, short drawers and sandals. His hair, cropped close to his head, revealed an elliptical skull. In his expressionless yellow face the thick lips were set under a hooked nose that emerged between jutting cheekbones. There was life only in the gray eyes and this life—watchful, solicitous, devoted—went out to the master.

"Go find Santos and tell him to come tomorrow to do whatever this gentleman wants done."

"Yes, *taita.*"

The Indian disappeared with rapid step which the slapping of his sandals repeated.

"I can let you use Santos only for a few days because we're plowing now and I need him," the old man explained.

Twilight slipped in through the broad door. The white wall took on a violet hue and the shadows began to thicken in the corners. The old man talked on slowly out of the experience of years, the number of which only he knew. The young man answered him briefly and to the point, in the face of his interlocutor's determination that he should weigh well everything he was saying.

The conversation was pleasant. Don Juan knew the life of the region through his own long, varied experience, and he talked of the past in the same language his forefathers might have used. In the rustic solitude of the highlands word passes from mouth to mouth and tales are handed down from father to son, and to the sons of sons in an unending chain. When the men of the uplands begin to talk, unsuspected traces of distant epochs appear in all their freshness and with their own flavor. The story is number, letter, page, book. But a living, moving book. It would be impossible to tell the things Don Juan had, to use his own expression, within his hand's grasp, and which he could describe to the last detail.

"Ah, sir," the old man went on, "this is a hard land. You are new here and you have to keep your eyes open."

The walls turned a mottled blue and finally black. The kerosene lamp in the middle of the table had to be lighted. A wan light filled the room, giving luster to the polished wood and making the dog's muzzle glisten. The shadows were motionless black masses in the corners and on the smoke-varnished roof, except where the chimney of the lamp projected a clear circle of light.

"Yes, of course," answered the engineer, "but you know how science has mastered everything."

"Certainly, that's true. But a man has to be wary and experienced out here," persisted the old man, lighting his cigarette over the lamp chimney. He took several puffs and went monotonously on.

"You've got to be on the lookout, sir."

"Yes, but it's just a question of going about things scientifically."

The wind suddenly burst into the room like a runaway pony with flying mane. Don Juan got up and shut the door, giving the old panels a bang, and then came back.

"Of course, sir, I understand. I studied at the school in Huamachuco, but science isn't always everything. I have seen young men like you come here, all full of plans and ideas, who returned to Lima in a little while, their buttocks raw and their bodies burned with erysipelas and the highland winds. They were walking calamities, sir. Others died. Yes, sir, the ones who ventured farther in, they died."

"Died," exclaimed Don Osvaldo, startled for a moment. And then recovering himself, with the imperturbable calm of the person prepared for any event, "But I won't die. I feel it in me that I shall triumph, and triumph I will."

"They died, sir, just as I said. I'll tell you how it was. . . ."

The old man leaned back in his chair. His long white beard gave him a Biblical air. Under the uneven shadow of his heavy brows, his eyes had a profound and penetrating gleam. The engineer pushed back his chair, crossed his legs and unfastened his collar. The minutes slipped by as the old man marshaled his memories. Silence hung heavy in the broad room.

"Mountain, jungle and river are cruel things, sir. Some years back three prospectors came through here. One was a Peruvian, Alejandro Lezcano, and the others were Poles. They were equipped with rifles, revolvers, maps, drawings, compasses, canned stuff and a whole load of knicknacks to trade with the Indians, for what they wanted to do was explore the forests of the Huayabamba, which, as you know, has its source near here and empties into the Huallaga. Everybody had great hopes in Lezcano as he had been educated in the United States. When he finished his studies he came back to this country, and went to Cajabamba to see his family. But fate had forged a chain of steel around him which he could not break: just then those foreigners showed up. First they became friends because they all knew English and then because Lezcano could meet them on equal terms in scientific matters. They talked their plans over with him and he decided to go with them, sharing first the hardships and then the profits of the expedition."

"What profits?"

"Oh, sir, they had a concession for the basin of the Huayabamba, one of the richest, where civilized man has hardly set his foot. Years ago, many years ago, there had been a road there, but it wasn't used any more and was all overgrown with jungle. Those were the days when there was trade with Pajatén, Pachiza, Uchiza and all those towns and with the Hibito and Cholón Indians. But the Indians began to kill people. The town of Pajatén disappeared, either because the Indians wiped it out or because people were afraid of them. Just imagine, my grandparents used to tell that these Indians would come out of their jungles to raid the towns of this province. In this way they completely destroyed Contumarca and Collai, killing the men and carrying off the women. It was a terrible thing, sir. And to make matters worse a flood carried away the bridge that had been built over one of the tributaries of the Huayabamba which is not navigable there, so you have to go on foot till you reach the place where a boat can travel. A relative of mine had the misfortune to find himself under those circumstances. He was coming home with a load of hats and all kinds of mountain herbs when he found that the bridge was no longer there. He waited for the river to fall and days went by and his supplies were gone. The Indian porters he had with him ran off and he was left alone there in the jungle and the rain kept on as though it were never going to stop. God be praised, the Indians did not kill him. All he had was a sack of corn and he had to eat it raw because it was raining so he could not build a fire. And even if it had cleared off, how was he going to start a fire when all the wood was soaking wet? I've been there myself, and I know what those things are like, sir. Well, as I was saying, my relative began to think how he was going to get out of his predicament. There was a tree growing there, a tree so big, he couldn't see the top. He had his axe with him, and he began to cut the tree so it would fall across the river and serve as a bridge. He spent days chopping away at the tree, eating his corn, and the rain never letting up. Finally the tree began to creak and then fell with a terrific crash. It lasted about an hour and it seemed as though the whole forest were coming down."

"Did he just imagine it or was it the echo?" asked the engineer.

"Oh, no, sir. The tree was so tall that it reached across to the other bank and brought down all the trees in its path. In the jungle one tree fells another and so it goes on for kilometers making a clearing in the denseness. It keeps this up until it comes to an open space in the forest, or a river, or a tree that is too big or deep-rooted. Whole villages and huts of the Indians have sometimes been crushed and, of course, the animals and wild beasts, too, and even the monkeys that skip from tree to tree."

"But you're forgetting about your relative there in the jungle," the young man reminded him banteringly.

"Oh, no. His time hasn't come yet. He got across on the huge trunk, but he had nothing left to eat. He made his way along those devilish paths as best he could, managing not to wander off the trail, and then he climbed up the side of the hills where the roads are nothing but a name, hanging on by the tree roots, rocks and bushes, until finally he reached the uplands. His clothes were in tatters, his shoes were torn to pieces, and his hands were raw wounds. He could not walk any farther and he collapsed. Some herders found him and carried him to their cabin but he could not keep food on his stomach. It was days before he got well. Meanwhile he had left his goods on the bank of the river and when he recovered he got some people to help him and went back for them. Everything was ruined. The animals had clawed the bundles open and torn everything to shreds."

"What about Lezcano and the others?" asked the engineer, holding his forehead between his hands and recalling the tales of Kipling that he had read. "I didn't think such things happened here in Peru, just around the mountain, as you might say. . . ."

"That was what I was going to tell you, sir. Those gentlemen hired guides from this part of the country, men who had been out before and who knew the region well. So they made their way into the jungle, confident and self-assured, because it was the so-called dry season. But in the jungle it rains hard or harder fourteen months a year. They found the tree that had served my relative as a bridge still there, but rotting away to return to the earth from which it had sprung. An army of red ants traveling back and forth was using the trunk as a bridge, too. Finally they reached the heart of the jungle, where all underfoot is mud, and the growth is so dense that they could not see the sun to get their bearings or even walk. The guides were of more use than the compasses, and they walked ahead, machete in hand, clearing a path for them. The rain was coming down in sheets, and even the thickest-foliaged tree was no protection against it. Can you imagine what it was like?"

"Of course, a difficult situation . . ."

"Yes, but it's one thing to imagine it and another to experience it. You have to have been among the wild animals, the insects, and the snakes and the never-ending rain to understand the torture they went through. But worst of all is the jungle itself, all that overpowering vegetation. Always that tormenting confusion, that inextricable mingling of primeval tree trunks, branches, brush, lianas, holding you back, catching you up, tripping you, imprisoning you. . . . They went along like this until one day they came to the edge of a river which was probably the Huayabamba."

"Why hadn't they traveled along the bank of one of its branches?" the engineer's logic argued.

"Sir, the small rivers have hardly any banks. The jungle begins right at their edge, and there are always bad spots to get through, and you have to climb up and down over the rocks that are frequent there, so it's just as bad and at times even worse than going right through the heart of the jungle. But there, beside the river, they found one of those huts the Indians use for a camp, and they could tell by the ashes of the fire that they had only recently left. The guides were frightened because the Hibitos must still be around there. Notwithstanding, the next day they went farther into the woods to find trees to make a boat, and then, when the time came, they stopped to eat their lunch. One of the guides said that not far from there was a brook and that was the place where the town of Pajatén used to be. There was nothing left of the town. The jungle had taken possession of it already, and the trees and creepers formed a gloomy shroud over the place where the houses had stood. The prospectors' spirits rose, for they said it was only twenty-five leagues to where the river joined the Huallaga and they could make it easily on the raft. Just then they heard footsteps among the leaves and through the foliage they caught sight of an Hibito who was hunting with a blowgun. The Indian would blow into the tube and the darts came out with such speed that you couldn't see them, just a dark wake through the air. The savage made off into the jungle, as though he were hunting birds, and gave no sign that he had noticed the strangers. His face was painted with *annatto,* and he wore a blue tunic, for they always dye the cloth they buy from the traders who go up the Huallaga that color."

"Did he intend to come back with more?" inquired the engineer as he saw that Don Juan was losing himself in the story of the Hibito.

"Probably, sir. They are savage Indians, and you

can't trust them as far as you can see them. They and the Cholones are always on the warpath against one another, and when they find a white man off his guard, they kill him, too. And even if he isn't off guard, if he has something they can steal. They are the laziest, meanest things you ever saw, mean, and they love to get drunk on that disgusting *masato* of theirs."

"Is that the stuff they make with saliva?"

"That's it, sir. To make it, they chew up yucca and put it in wooden troughs, with enough water to ferment. That's *masato*. Would you believe that I have drunk it and liked it?"

"Do you mean it?"

"Yes, sir. I call it disgusting now, but there was a time, and then many times when it did not seem so. The first time was once when I was going through the Huallaga. When you go down you use a canoe, for the Indians are very good at steering through narrows and shooting rapids. But coming back the canoe can't ascend them, so you have to go overland and portage. One day we were almost ready to drop, with the canoe on our shoulders, in that hell of rocks and creepers. I was so tired I couldn't take another step. An Indian offered me a gourd of *masato* and I drank and drank and drank. It didn't seem dirty or disgusting. It was sweet and refreshing. I drank and drank . . . and after that I always used it when I was in the jungles. When I think about it now I laugh at my squeamishness."

The engineer made no comment and the old man fell silent for a moment. They were both thinking that when faced by primeval savage nature man unconsciously comes to imitate her, and there comes a moment when even carrion is good if it can prolong life in its struggles with a medium that admits of no bargaining or invasions.

"Well, sir," the old man went on, "the guides did not want to stay in the jungle any longer. Besides they were sick of being food for vampire bats. There are so many of them and they are so voracious that they will attack even men, especially on nights when there is no moon. When the moon is up, if you sleep in the moonlight the bats won't bother you. But darkness is their ally, and there's no lack of darkness in the jungle. When they woke up after those dark nights they would have two or three wounds on their neck and feet. Those animals will suck the blood even out of the wild birds or the chickens those heathens raise."

The engineer spoke up, with all the piety of a former student of the Colegio de la Recoleta in Lima: "Heathen? I notice that you have been calling them heathen. Don't they believe in God?"

"Who can say, sir? . . . They believe that God is the tallest tree or the biggest river, and they have their ceremonies and their witch doctors. If they become Christians it's for what they can get out of it. Years ago missionaries used to go among them and make them gifts to win them over, because their sermons—especially when they had to use an interpreter—were not very successful. The Indians found the mysteries of the Immaculate Conception and the Blessed Trinity very hard to understand and even more difficult that a man should let himself be killed to save others. An Hibito would receive a knife, a mirror and some glass beads if he would allow his son to be baptized. . . . The next day he would come back with the child to have it baptized over again."

"But, Don Juan, you never finished the story about the prospectors," laughed the engineer.

"Neither do you stop asking questions and making remarks. You need more explanations than the souls in purgatory, prayers. All right, you just be patient and I'll finish. In spite of all the offers the prospectors made them the guides went back, leaving them there with their Winchesters, their revolvers, their maps, their plans, their canned food, their compasses, and their trinkets. . . ."

"And?"

"And they were never heard of again. They never

reached the other side, where there are towns in which white people live, nor did they ever again appear on this side. That's the jungle, sir."

The young engineer was turning the matter over carefully in his mind and he sat for a long time in thoughtful silence. Don Juan watched him from the vantage point of his years, and he was not surprised to hear him say: "Of course, if they had used system. . . ."

"Just as you please, sir. But out here you have to learn what the place itself teaches you. Who can save you from the bite of a snake or the aim of a blowgun? What defense have you against the maze of the jungle, the current ready to engulf you or the chasm that opens at your feet and makes you giddy so you will fall into it?"

"You just wait and see, Don Juan, I'm going to do something big and fine around here."

Don Juan, like the sly old fox he was, asked as though he were not in the least interested: "Well now, and what is it you are planning to do?"

"What you've told me about the jungle and the Huayabamba basin has aroused my curiosity and it may lead to something worth while. They say there are mines in this part of the country. They may be there. It's a matter of finding out."

"You see, friend, you haven't made up your mind yet. Afterward I'll hear what you have to say. Go up to Campana Ridge, friend, and from there you can see first . . . afterward you can explore all you like, but keep your eyes open. Are you planning to go to Bambamarca? All right, as soon as you get there, say that you don't feel well."

"Are you making fun of me, Don Juan?"

"I was never more serious in my life. Those Indians at Bambamarca are very touchy and they take offense at anything. The mayor or the governor will receive you warmly and treat you well, for, no question about it, they are very hospitable. Very well, they will serve you a big gourd plate of potatoes and a big bowl of soup, and another plate full of ocas. You have to eat it all up, because unless you do they won't give you any more food. They can't imagine that everybody hasn't the same appetite as themselves, so if he doesn't finish all the food they think he does it to slight them. So, right from the start, ask for balm mint or orange-blossom tea, which they always get at Calemar, and say that you suffer very much with your stomach. If you do this, even though you don't eat much, everything will go along smoothly."

The engineer laughed tolerantly and indulgently. He had already been told these Indians were stupid, but there were good times ahead, even for them.

"You can take my word for it, Don Juan, that with the plans I have in mind for this region even their habits will change. Another thing I can't stand is their chewing coca. Let them smoke it if they want to but not chew it. That plant keeps them stupified and in a daze. I think a big part of the Indian and half-breed psychology comes from that. Years and years they have been sapping their vitality. . . ."

"No doubt, sir. Look, I would advise you to stick to the river, to the Marañón. Why don't you pan gold? There's a mint of wealth there, just waiting to be taken out. If I weren't an old man, I'd be down there doing it myself, but the climate and the insects would be too much for me now. . . ."

"You just wait and see, Don Juan, this is going to make history."

An old Indian woman with skin the color of the earth slipped into the room with the wind. She seemed a scrap of shadow in her black clothes. Her back bowed with years, her hands clasped together and her gaze fixed on the floor, she announced, in a voice hard to define, that dinner was ready. Then she slipped back into the night.

"Well, I would be very glad . . . very glad, indeed. But mountain, jungle and river are cruel things, sir."

With the thought of the jungle tantalizing him, the engineer set off toward the mountains at the break of day. He had to climb to the top of that ridge which was discernible through the raveled fleece of clouds to survey the region and draw up his plans. Mines? Jungles? To tame and civilize this wild, luxuriant nature they would have to organize a powerful company which would build roads, set up machinery to make available its timber, mines, fruits, gold, everything that was spread out before the hand of man who would not even take the trouble to reach for it.

His guide was an Indian, as dark and rugged as the mountains themselves, who walked at a steady unchanging pace ahead of the sorrel the engineer was riding. The latter tried to draw him into conversation, but the Indian answered briefly, as he kept steadily dipping into his lime gourd and chewing his satisfying coca. The visitor made conversation as he rode along, taking note of the fact that a harmony exists between man and nature, and so, in the valley, man chatters away like the river and the trees, and as he ascends the uplands he becomes taciturn like them. They met a man from Bambamarca, who was coming down driving a pair of hairy asses.

"Where are you from?"

"Bambamarca, *taita*."

"You on your way to the Marañón?"

"Yes, *taita*."

"Going to get coca or bananas?"

"Yes, *taita*."

"Is it going to rain today?"

The Indian looked up at the sky, turning his head in all directions.

"Hardly think so, *taita*."

The engineer touched his sorrel with the spur and overtook the guide, who had walked ahead. Thinking to make him talk a little more he said: "Why don't the people from Bambamarca want to talk?"

"That's the way they are, *taita*."

"What about you?"

"Me too, I guess, *taita*."

The Indian from the ranch kept the secret of the

community Indian and his own as well. He knows that they talk long and merrily, but not with white people. The minute they see a light face or clothing different from their own they put a seal on their lips and open them only to answer in the fewest possible words. Only the family groups that gather by the door of their huts, or the community when it comes together about the threshing floor or the fields, hear their comments on the happenings of the day or their pleasant tales. Then the talk is of the sorrow of the plants withering in the drought, or how the lake turns red in memory of the death in the olden days of many warriors who were beheaded and thrown into its waters for rising against their oppressors. Or what the sun says as the clouds pass across it and how the claps of thunder are produced by St. Isidore, the patron saint of farmers, who, mounted on a fiery, iron-shod steed, gallops across the sky ordering the good rain. Or for instance, that marvelous tale of a certain Tungurbao who appeared near Chuquitén and nobody knew where he came from nor where he went to. But he stayed around there for a long time, playing his flute of gold on the nights when the moon was full, luring and seducing the girls with the charm of his music, so beautiful, so clear, so piercing that it filled the whole valley and has never been heard before or since. Perhaps Tungurbao disappeared because he could not bear the tears of the girls' mothers, or because his pact with the Devil had come to an end. This happened long ago, many, many years back. . . .

The crest of Campana Ridge reached up against the sky.

The travelers left to one side the village of Bambamarca huddled beside a smooth-surfaced lake in which the little houses with their curving stone walls and sharp-ridged roofs were reflected, and began to climb a difficult trail. The vegetation had become different, too. Bushes were less frequent, planted fields grew scarcer, and on both sides of the trail grew high yellow grass, spangled with bright drops of water. It was cold now, and the wind seared their lips.

The rocks showed their sharp ridges beside the road, and below in the canyon. The sorrel had to make its way up this tortuous route which rose and fell and was as slippery as soap. Every now and then they saw small cows in between the rocks, nibbling at the hard, brittle *ichu* grass. The sorrel began the calvary of an animal new to the mountains. It slipped and fell and stopped to look—both horse and rider—fearfully at the chasms, which began to gape beside the perpendicular slabs of rock. And then up once more, step by step, curve by curve, from rock to rock. How long? Forever. Whoever expects to get anything from the mountains must be prepared to suffer.

The engineer turned his head to look back. Down below the little village of Bambamarca had shrunk to the size of a child's plaything. The men moved about like ants and the blue lake was but an eye through which the earth gazed upon the immensity of the mountains.

But a heavy fog was rolling up and hiding everything from view. In a little while village, hills, sky, road were only recollections shrouded in white fleece. The guide close ahead in his dark poncho was a blur.

"If it keeps on like this we won't be able to see a thing."

The Indian answered briefly: "It's always like this in the morning. Later it will clear."

And he kept on adding lime and coca to the wad in his cheek. The engineer was nervously alert to the stumbling and falling of his horse. Suddenly, through the woolly curtain of mist came a mournful song and the bleating of sheep. A shepherdess and her flock were near by, and it gave the young man a queer sensation to realize that he was surrounded by living creatures of whom he was aware only by their sound.

> "Pretty, pretty condor,
> Do not steal my little lamb,
> Do not steal my little lamb."

It was a thin little voice which floated on the air with a tone of sorrow and supplication, and which rose in anger without losing its melancholy air:

> "Because if you steal it
> You will be the first to die.
> You will be the first to die."

A feeling of sadness crept over Don Osvaldo. The throbbing sorrow of these songs was contagious. They voiced the tribulation that welled from the deepest springs of a long-suffering, patient race, victim alike of a pitiless serfdom and of the savage, heartless mountains. These songs were the offspring of hunger and lash, of crag and wild beast, of snow and fog, of loneliness and wind.

The song was left behind, lost in the distance, for they were still climbing. But it was not the rough steepness of the path that made them aware of this, for stone steps had been cut there and the out-croppings of the rock rubbed against the stirrups. Fog, fog. There was no longer even hay. Alongside the path wide flat-leaved plants huddling close to the earth were barely visible. Fog. Yes, one had to accustom one's eyes to it. Don Osvaldo could see that the rocks were black and blue, and that the layers of stone were piling up in ever rougher, more shapeless masses. The path disappeared among the stones and slabs of rock, and the guide stopped.

"We'll have to leave the horse, he won't be able to make it here."

They tied the sorrel to a high rock and he whinnied nervously as the men left and disappeared into the fog.

Soft sandals were better than hobnailed boots there where the rocks spread out their broad slanting surfaces, or broke up into shale or sharp pebbles which afforded a treacherous footing. The engineer slipped at every step, and the guide had to keep close beside him or he would have fallen and been dashed to pieces

on the rocks of the perilous slope. The young man's
ears began to buzz. It was a pair of cold stiff hands
that the guide clasped between his own. It was hard
to breathe. It was almost as though there were no air.

"Hadn't we better go back?"

"Just the least little bit more and we'll be there."

They kept on, catching hold of projecting fragments
of rock. The mist persistently hid the precipices, which
seemed even more terrifying because it was impossible
to see to the bottom. One last effort, pulling themselves
up by their hands and their feet and they were on a
bare ridge along which the guide moved calling upon
his memory, his eyes alert to every fissure and pinnacle.
They walked on a little farther, the young man's legs
numb with fatigue, until they reached a black peak in
the crevices of which the snow had frozen, making a
rough glittering design of crystal.

"Here it is, *taita*."

"The summit?"

"Yes, *taita*."

Don Osvaldo came up beside the guide and sat
down. The mist was splitting up into broad curtains
that billowed about in the wind. The icy breath of the
mountains tugged at the Indian's poncho, attempting
to tear it away, and drove stilettos of cold into the
engineer through his heavy sweater. He felt his heart
pounding in an anguish of distress, and his temples
throbbed as though they were about to burst as a
shudder ran through him from head to foot. A stream
of blood spurted from his nose, and in a rage of terror
he burst out: "Have you brought me here to kill me,
you Indian devil?"

The Indian would have run off if he had not seen the
revolver.

"You dumb, filthy, stupid Indian," the engineer
raved on, while the handkerchief he held in his trembling hands turned red.

"It's the *soroche,* the mountain sickness, *taita.* The
altitude. . . . Chew some coca."

And he held out to him the striped pouch in which

he carried the fine-cut leaf. Don Osvaldo took a handful and chewed it hurriedly. Lime, too, without losing any time.

The sun had come out, near at hand, but cold. It glowed majestically above the clouds which were piled up below and driven swiftly along by the wind. As soon as the young man began to swallow the bittersweet juice he closed his eyes because nothing any longer impinged on his senses. A quiet languor came over him and he was only dimly aware of two human silences in the midst of the vast cosmic silence. Was this death?

No, it was not. He had raised his eyes to the east and an overwhelming sense of awe brought him slowly to his feet. Over there, toward the rising sun, partly hidden by spindrift clouds, lay a black unending sea. Campana Ridge, on which they were standing, descended in sharp spurs until it was lost in the rippling mass of darkness, thick and deep, silent and vast, in whose bosom the rays of the sun lost their sheen. It was a sea of night. It was the jungle.

On the horizon the sky seemed to limit it with a mass of leaden clouds, but one felt that this darkness did not end there, that it spread out to cover the face of an unsuspected world whose limits man could never guess from the outside.

The engineer said to himself, "It is the jungle," and his words echoed strangely in the silence and he trembled in every fiber of his body and soul as he became aware of the paradox of this black splendor.

A pale streak that was barely discernible and which lost itself in that vast night of the day was a river. How many century-old trees there must have been, their boughs crowding one another in a relentless determination to live. And if they had fallen—as Don Juan related—plowing furrows through the denseness, they soon would be covered over by the crowding growth that spread itself through space and time, since it must ever supersede and overcome time. That was the jungle.

The engineer would have liked to voice his emotions and he turned his eyes to the guide, who stood there as mute and impassible as the rocks. Like the rocks that go on and on, toward the north, forming a countless wild, majestic series of battlements. Callangate and the brilliant snow-crowned Cajamarquilla, silent and erect with the assured pride of giants, commanded the chain of mountains that went on until they disappeared from sight.

And could their beginnings be seen? The same negative answer came from the south, for the ranges wound in and out, showing their sharp peaks without ever giving a hint of where they started. On their slopes the farms were little spots that could hardly be made out. Bambamarca seemed a heap of pebbles and man and beast were swallowed up by the immensity and the distances. On the horizon there was always the sky with its theatrical clouds that looked like scenery. And to the west, the same stone giants reared their sharp rude ridges into the region where men looked in search of God.

And between the ranges, between these mountains to the west and to the east, far down, a great white swath crawled like a serpent at their base, joining them together and guiding them in their headlong flight. It was the Marañón, a river as great as the mountains and the jungle. Occasionally the bulge of a slope hid it from view, but never for long. The ribbon appeared again and again, unwinding its broad curves until it disappeared behind Cajamarquilla, though leaving behind the assurance that it did not end there, but went on until it stopped of its own free will.

"Mountains, jungle and river are cruel things, sir."

And eternal.

5

Many Fish and an Otter

The river kept sinking and sinking and it was no trouble at all for us and old Matías to ferry travelers across. No log jams came down now. Even Roge's light raft was as useful as anybody's. The summer truce had come, as gently as the foam along the riverbank.

As the water dropped back to its old level, it left behind inlets on the banks that were a delight. We put fish traps in them. The old man was as happy as a child setting the funnels of reeds or wild cane in midcurrent and there was not a fish that got past them. In the pools at the foot of the rocks we fished with dynamite. It takes skill to do this well. First you throw in pieces of cooked yucca and meat. The fish are attracted by the food and more and more of them keep coming. Suddenly you throw in a charge of dynamite. They see the white fuse and the gray cartridge and swarm toward it, when suddenly the bait explodes and leaves them floating on the water belly up. You have to be a good swimmer to get to them in the current, and work fast, too, to throw them on the bank, for they slip away, like quicksilver. Once they get out of the pool, it's only the big ones we go after.

We spent all our time at these things. I didn't do a stroke of work in my banana grove and Don Matías didn't ever get started on his gold-washing at Recodo del Lobo. And what about Arturo and Rogelio?

The old man said: "The boys have gone on a tear, I'm sure. If the river keeps on falling, it's going to be dangerous for them to get past La Escalera. I like to see it fall, but not this much."

That brought La Escalera to my mind and I began to think seriously about it. It is a long stretch where the river runs over a bed of sharp stones, and is bordered by rocks chiseled flush to form a narrow passageway, like a strait. The stones jut up like awls, and you have to work your way through them and all the while the water is roaring and boiling so you can't hear a word or even a shout. If there are more than four on a raft, they appoint one the chief boatman. He stands or squats in the middle of the raft, to chart the course, shouting, "Left," "Right," "Pull hard," and nothing else. The boatmen sink their paddles with all their strength into the rushing water, kneeling on the edge of their rafts in a kind of primitive prayer to the forces of Nature. When the river is high, it covers the rocks, and the difficulty is to avoid crashing on the jutting turn as you come out and to steer clear of the reefs along the edge. But the current is so strong that the danger of a crash and the unlashing of the raft as a result is almost inevitable. For this reason it is better to wait until the waters fall a little. Once past La Escalera, there is no danger. A fellow can drift along on his raft, stretched out, his own boss, chewing his coca and smoking, watching the trees along the bank drift by, and the crags covered with cactus and the screeching flocks of parrots flapping their wings in a green vibration.

I said to Don Matías: "They'll be along. Arturo is one of the best boatmen I ever knew and Roge can get by swimming."

The old man agreed, "Yes, I guess you're right."

He said no more but he looked me in the eye, proud of his race, calling attention to the fact that he was the father of such sons.

Meanwhile we kept on fishing to our heart's content. One has to take advantage of an opportunity like this when the fish are plentiful, for in the summer the inlets and pools disappear and the water goes back to the channel it has cut for itself through so many long years. Then we have to use hooks to catch a tasteless little fish, though, to tell the truth, one can always get them for, as the water is clear, they can see the bait a long way off.

We were fishing in a deep pool that had formed in a hollow on the beach and which was fed by a branch of the river. It was full of *boquichicos* which were swimming around trying to hide. Just wait till we get the dynamite.

"Look how many Encarnitas. . . . Look how many Encarnitas," said the old man in fun.

It was his own joke. This kind of fish has a very big mouth, and so *boquichico* (small mouth) was the nickname of Encarna, that *cholo* who lives at the end of the valley and has a mouth that stretches from ear to ear. When he comes to Don Matías's house, the old man calls out to his wife: "Melcha, fry us a *boquinada* (no mouth)." And somebody among those present says: *"Boquinada?"* And the old man answers, winking his eye: "Oh, yes, because now you can't call it by its real name." The others laugh, and Encarna pretends he has not heard a word. The old man likes such tricks.

Don Matías was standing by the edge of the pool, wearing nothing but a pair of drawers, when suddenly he let out a shout and dived into the water head first like a duck. The water, which was already roiled with the mud from the bottom, was churned up still darker, but he could be seen moving like a crab after a dark mass. It got away from him, swam upstream, and came out in one of the branches. It was a light brown otter and was covered with its characteristic gelatinous substance which glistens in the sun. The old man was close behind it, and I jumped into the branch to head it off. When it saw that it was between the two of us, it leaped to the bank to jump into the river in front. Otters cannot run on rocks except under water, especially if they are hot from the sun, as these were, so the old man quickly caught it. First it slipped out of his grasp, and then as he managed to get hold of it again the animal buried its teeth in the palm of his hand. All this happened as quick as a flash of lightning. The old man grabbed it by one leg, making it loosen its hold in the struggle, then whirled it into the air and brought it down, smashing its head on the rocks. The otter gave a convulsive shudder and died.

Don Matías was sucking his wound and said, laughing as he looked at the animal stretched out full length: "I'll give the skin to Roge and he can sell it."

And he went on laughing, and digging his toe into the otter's slack belly: "You devil. Trying to steal people's food from them, weren't you?"

The blood from his wound was dripping on the stones. Suddenly he turned pale.

"Does your hand hurt?"

"I can't say exactly," he muttered, "just a feeling that came over me. . . ."

And he looked at the river which was not at all threatening. On the contrary, its waters kept falling and rippling quietly along. The old man's gaping mouth was twisted in a painful grimace.

I picked up the animal and we started home. We did not say a word on the way, nor when we got there and not even as we skinned the otter. We salted the hide and the sun dried it quickly. It was pliant and silky and it was a pleasure to stroke it, but Don Matías would not even look at it.

6

La Escalera

Arturo and Roge were having a high time in Shicún.
They seemed to think that all the rum in the valley
had been distilled just for them. Venancio Landauro
received them as cordially as he always did, and from
the moment they got there they began drinking the hot
liquor that takes away sorrow. Which sorrows? You
can always find them, especially if the object is to get
rid of them. There is always some little sorrow sticking in the throat like a fishbone which you can wash
down with a drink.

While singing voices and happy eyes gave the lie
to sorrows, they caroused about first in one place and
then another, towing along with them a group of
cholos, drunk like themselves and, like them, good
boatmen, trying out the liquor to see if it was good.

The visitors walked along the paths that zigzagged
between the yellow cane fields, swaying a little in spite
of the friendly hands that held them up. Roge began a
song with which he had consoled himself in the town
of Cajamba, once when he got into a fight there with
the odds against him and from which he emerged with
part of his clothes missing:

"Boatman of Calemar,
Stranger in a far land.

72

Poor stranger,
Only a poncho and no hat."

The end of the song rippled through the rum which
he was holding ready to his hot lips. It gurgled against
the neck of the bottle or the round rim of the gourd:
"On-ly po-o-ncho and no-o ha-at."

The other *cholos* laughed, and Arturo broke in:
"But all us folks from the valley are brothers, ain't that
so?"

"Sure, man, sure, what a question," came the en-
thusiastic chorus. Without a hat, and sometimes without even a poncho the brothers went weaving along.
Their boon companions had taken charge of their garments, for they no longer knew what was going on.

"In the fields there grows a flower
Which they call the holy thistle.
Why do you never notice me
When I love you so."

Just then a fine-looking *cholita* came by, wearing
a gay percale skirt, her cheeks as rosy as an angel's
and eyes that looked as though they had been rubbed
in with a sooty finger. The jaws of the fellows from
Calemar dropped open as they stopped to look after
her. They were going to say something when one of
the others spoke up: "Careful, careful, she's branded."

One of the *cholos* of the group was already showing his teeth, like a dog getting ready for a fight, but
they behaved themselves and there was no occasion
for knives to come into play.

When they woke up after a long sleep, still half-
drunk, they decided to start down the river. They had
managed to bargain the price of the raft down to
twenty-five *soles* and they set out shouting noisy fare-
wells. As they floated down they were happy with their
fine raft, made of fifteen stout, straight logs, lashed
with withes which are better than wire or rope because they neither rust nor rot. Their equipment lay

in the middle of the raft: sweetened corn meal porridge in rough baskets fashioned from cane leaves; bananas, jugs of rum; saddlebags; ponchos; all dry, because the raft was a good one. You only had to look at it!

"Good-bye . . . Good-bye," shouted the Shicún *cholos*.

Arturo and Roge answered waving their paddles which they used only now and then to steer with. The raft was light, high and curving at the prow, narrowing at the stern, and she behaved as though she had been trained. The first curve wiped out the friendly crowd of *cholos* who had gathered at the wharf and were shouting themselves hoarse. Alone and face to face for the first time in many days, Arturo and Roge hardly knew what to say to each other, perhaps because they had so much to say. Something had sprung up between them, something impalpable, but real and threatening. The truth of the matter was that Arturo had gone along so as not to lose face for Roge had been boasting and bragging and refusing to listen to any advice, saying that taking La Escalera was like falling off a log for them.

Just for something to say Roge remarked: "A good raft, this is."

"It ought to be. It cost good money."

The raft drifted along with a steady balance. Two or three strokes of the paddles carried them through the little whirlpools and the load did not get wet. Arturo was an expert at breaking up the waves with a stroke and twist of his paddle. No matter how big the wave was, it was completely undone by the time it reached the raft, humiliated and as though fawning at the raft's feet before disappearing altogether. The river went straight for a while, then curved, then zigzagged in and out, but the current was not too strong and the boatmen could enjoy the view of the banks where *higuerones* and *gualangos* grew, or the rocks where silent, naked cactuses showed their round blood-red flowers. The parrots flew noisily overhead, and oc-

casionally a deer, which had come down to the bank
to drink or enjoy the shade, dashed off and went leaping madly from rock to rock until it was lost from
sight.

"They're the devil's own spawn," remarked Rogelio.

Arturo said nothing and went on chewing his coca
with his eyes fixed on the point where the waters disappeared behind the jutting crags. He could not even
see the trail down which they had come years ago with
Lucinda, winding like a thread over the slopes of the
hills until it lost itself along the banks. If he looked at
the raft—he was sitting in the prow on the roll of rope
they used to tie up—his gaze remained fixed on the
water that passed gurgling under the light poles.

Rogelio understood his concern and asked him:
"What about La Escalera?"

Arturo, turning his head to look at his brother who
was in the back steering, thought for a moment and
then answered: "If we go through today it will be
around sundown, but the river is neither high nor low.
Look . . ."

Just then they passed close to a cliff that projected
into the water. Arturo pointed out:. "When the water
around this cliff doesn't reach that top notch, it's bad
business. And if it isn't low enough so you can see
the blue stones, it is worse. Right now it's bad; it's between the two."

Rogelio answered: "But we'll get through all right,
man. . . . We'll get through."

"It's not so easy," insisted Arturo. "By vespers it's
pretty dark there. Take a look at the sun . . . in a place
as narrow as that it's not very light even during the day.
Look at the sun, man."

It was about four o'clock and the sun no longer
shone on the river. A reddish light reached halfway
down the cliffs, and below they lay in shadow which
picked out the profile of the peaks on the other side.
Arturo went on.

"It would be better to go ashore on that little spit
we're coming to, tie up the raft and spend the night

there. I know what I'm talking about, brother, I've been through it eight times."

But Roge would not be persuaded: "Bah, I thought you were a good boatman. Let's go on. We'll get through all right, man."

Arturo did not argue with him any more. He did not want to seem like a coward to his younger brother, but the blowhard was certainly going to get a lesson. As he added fresh coca to the wad in his mouth—coca between the jaws of the *cholos* helps them through the bad hours as well as the good—he merely muttered: "All right, man."

They became silent. A wall of irritation had sprung up between them. To Arturo his brother seemed a show-off who did not know what he was talking about; and Roge returned the compliment, considering Arturo a coward who backed out when things got difficult. They did not even talk about what had to be done. To be sure, it was not much. A stroke of the paddle to one side or the other and the raft changed its course as gracefully as a flying heron. The orange light spread over the vertical peaks and up the slopes while the sun went down on the other side. The shadows began creeping up immediately afterward, firm and unyielding. They rose in a heavy mass as though from the river itself, seeming determined to wipe out the cliffs and leave the waters alone with the night.

From ahead a loud noise was carried back to them on the wind. Arturo turned his head quickly: "You hear that? It's La Escalera. We've still got time to go ashore. It's pretty dark already."

But Roge held out stubbornly. The figure of Florinda was dancing before his eyes. Just wait until she found out the risks he had taken, going through the dangerous shallows and at night, just to get back to her? His answer was slow in coming and the raft and the minutes drifted on.

"Come on, man. Aren't we supposed to be boatmen? Come on."

Arturo, kneeling in the bow, picked up his paddle

firmly and held it poised in the air. Rogelio imitated him. It was too late now to think of landing. The raft had entered into the current.

"To the left," shouted Arturo, "hard, man."

The paddles cleaved the waters to the right powerfully, steering the raft away from some rocks which loomed up like the scouts of an ambush party. The raft rocked over the rough waves and the current was powerful. To one side and the other the white foam showed where the river broke over the rocks along the side. The noise was getting louder and from farther downstream came a menacing roar.

"To the right, to the right."

Once more the paddles plunged in violently, as though to punish the rebellious waters. The raft managed to skim over a rock as sharp as a chisel.

Danger had wiped out the last rough edge of unpleasantness between the brothers, and they were deeply linked together again. Once more they were two men struggling against the common enemy, joined in a bond of union that only danger can engender. They were united like two warriors in the face of the enemy who was right there, under those poles that held them above the water with the ease of a giant's hand.

"Watch it, man, here she comes . . . La Escalera."

And they could see and hear the water rushing noisily between a hundred sharp rocks that projected above it. They had to row hard to keep out of the cascades that formed on the sides. Arturo's sharp eyes peered into the shadows in search of the course to steer. He found it. Straight down the middle. Rogelio rowed along in silence with ears alert. Both felt within their own breasts the savage boiling of La Escalera. They were about a quarter of a mile from the rocky tumult when, suddenly, their paddles dipped uselessly in the water which flowed past without carrying them along, and the raft came to rest in the middle of the river with disquieting stubbornness. Arturo looked around at the cliffs and there they were, silent as ever, looking on as though in contempt. Rogelio raised his eyes and at a glance took in his brother's dismayed expression. Then he, too, looked up at the cliffs: it was a fact, they were not moving an inch. The cliffs stood before them, cold and motionless. The water ran past as though it had nothing to do with them, as if they and the raft were suspended in the air. But they were not in the air—if only they were!—and the raft just rocked a little, barely moving. Finally Arturo turned toward Rogelio.

"We're stuck, man."

Not a word did he answer. He realized that it was his fault, and he could not bring himself to acknowledge it and ask forgiveness. He threw his paddle into the middle of the raft and let himself fall heavily on the logs. Arturo sat down and pulled out his pouch to add more coca to the big wad he already had in his mouth. Meanwhile it was growing dark. The waters kept flowing by, breaking against the cliffs farther down as they go on their way to Calemar. The waters would have taken them there, but now they went past alone.

What Arturo feared had happened. The water had not been low enough to show all the rocks nor high enough so the raft could float over them, and so they were stuck there. The next day, with more light, he could have seen the big waves that formed over the high rocks and passed to one side, but there was no point now in upbraiding Roge for his stubbornness. The only thing that bothered him now was that it was not going to be easy to get out of there. The water was too deep for him to find bottom and pry the raft loose. Feeling through one of the spaces between the logs he could tell that the raft was skewered on the point of the rock. To get off there was not a matter for men. It was a matter for God. If only the river would rise . . . God was the river.

The brothers had been watching one another, silently, out of the corner of their eyes till night closed in upon them. Rocked on the swaying raft they had heard the water run past, hour after hour. This noise had silenced the sound of the incessant movement of the lime gourds. As soon as it became possible they looked at one another again, as day broke forming a milky layer far, far up, against the heavily clouded-over, hope-bearing sky. That's why they say God's in His Heaven!

7

Days That Try the Soul

"How long before the river will rise," sighed Arturo despondently.

Those were dark days for the men, with the cliffs pressing in on them from the front, the waters roaring past with an echo of death and the raft swaying back and forth in a relentless rhythm—yes—no . . . yes—no . . . yes—no . . . and always remaining in the same spot, caught fast on the jagged edge of Fate. Despair raged and writhed in their breasts like a serpent coiling to strike.

Rogelio, who felt that he was to blame for their predicament, repeated his intention of jumping into the river to reach that cliff on the left which showed crevices and looked as though it could be climbed. If he could get to the top he could go to Shicún or Calemar or climb to the uplands where the Indians live and get a rescue party to save his brother. Arturo still opposed the idea even though the river was not rising and the wind was perversely sweeping the clouds away.

They had eaten all the bananas they were carrying and their supply of rum was dwindling. About noon, when the sun stood between the cliffs, it blazed down on them unmercifully. They dipped their hats into the river and poured the muddy water over their hot, tan-

gled hair under which their brains felt as though they
were in a fiery furnace. They tried drinking the water
but it left a film of mud in their mouths and they went
back to the rum.

Roge was drunk, and he threw an empty gourd into
the water. The yellow sphere rode down on the waves
and he shouted after it:

"Flori . . . Florinda . . . There goes my farewell to
you."

Not even an echo answered. The waters roared
through La Escalera which bristled with menacing
rocks. If only the rise in the river would come, they
would know how to get by them. The waters were
still falling as the afternoon descended, and the raft
tilted backward depriving them of even the comfort
of resting on a level surface.

On the fifth night, very late, they felt the raft straight-
en out again. Their sharp ears caught the thud of the
logs against the rocks. They crouched there in silence.
In the darkness they would not be able to steer and it
would mean certain death. The raft rocked heavily
back and forth, there was a crash, as though something
had hit it and become enmeshed in it, a tree probably,
but it went by quickly, catching here and there, and the
framework moved lazily up and down right where it
was.

The new day came without bringing any change, just
the muddy foul-smelling water flowing past. And, again,
as the hours went by, the slow tilting of the raft made it
impossible to move or rest because of the danger of
falling in the water. And another day and another. The
men were as silent as the rocks and the only sound
was that of the water which roared and swirled below,
filled with a fierce thirst for destruction. The men's
thick lips were stained with the bright green of the coca
they were chewing and at the corners of their mouths
there was a white film of lime.

One night Roge got very drunk and began muttering
words which Arturo could not make out.

"A little handful, brother, mine's all gone. Give

me the jug, man. Haven't we anything stronger? Tomorrow I'm going to jump in the water. Listen, if I die you tell that girl Florinda that it was for the sake of seeing her. Remember."

Arturo moved over to him and shook him by the shoulders. He shouted in his ear: "Don't drink any more. Pull yourself together. You're going to fall in the water."

Rogelio quieted down a little and flung himself upon the raft. By morning his brother was worn out from holding him on by the shoulders all night. He wanted to rest a little and, shaking him, he said to encourage him: "Look, the river is rising."

Roge sat up quickly, giving a bound like a cat, and looked on every side with his bleared eyes. He realized that it was not true, and he muttered "Don't fool me, man."

But he did not lie down again. He kept looking angrily at the water with an expression of defiance and despair. All that was left was two gourds of rum and half a knapsack of coca from which they filled their pouches hourly as they became empty. The baskets of toasted corn porridge had not even been touched, because they had coca which is better. The damned river which will not rise and will carry water but not the raft! With sips of rum they whiled away the despair of the long hours. Once more the sun came up to sink its claws into their bodies, worn out by thirst and hunger, lack of sleep, and the unbroken tension of danger.

Roge got to his feet, moving his arms energetically and said to his brother: "Listen, man, the water is going to hold us here till we are dead. Even if the river rises we won't have the strength to row. I think the best thing to do is for me to jump into the river and see if I can get ashore. I can climb up that cliff and get out."

"No, listen, brother, don't do that. Those crevices in it are high up and the current is strong."

"If it should carry me along, I'll make for the middle and swim downstream, for the current goes right through La Escalera."

"No, man, the current will drag you along, for on that side it is very strong and it will throw you upon the rocks and into the eddies."

"I'm going to jump, you'll see how I'll make it all right."

Arturo sorrowfully watched his brother fasten his pants tighter and tie his pouch of coca and his lime gourd around his neck in his bandanna. He caught him by the shoulders in a movement that was both rough and tender.

"No, Rogito. . . . Don't jump, man."

A white heron passed overhead flying slowly and gracefully. It disappeared around a bend. It was heading for life.

And Roge, slipping out of his hands, shouted: "I'm going . . . I'm going."

And he leaped sidewise into the river, cutting through the water, using his shoulder as a keel. This carried him forward a considerable distance and he began to swim arm over arm. He cut through the water vigorously. Arturo kept his eyes fixed on him and each rise and fall of his panting chest breathed anxiety. He called out: "Hurry, hurry!"

He knew that Roge would not be able to climb out by the cliff, because the crevices were too high and he wanted him, when he realized this, to make for the middle of the river before the current dragged him down into the whirlpools. So he had to get as far up as he could.

"Hurry, hurry!"

Roge had not heard him but it was as though he had. He was very near. He had reached the side of the cliff without going very far down. He stretched out his arms but he could not reach the crevices and meanwhile the current was tugging at him. He clasped at the rough surface of the rock, trying to hold on, but the current was too strong. Finally he found a jutting angle to which he clung with his bleeding, scratched hands. He flexed his legs trying to make a leap and reach the crevices but he could not do it. He turned and looked at his brother. It was impossible for him to get back to the raft. They were both taking stock of the situation and they were aware of the same thing. All the while the current tugged at Roge as though it were trying to pull him loose with its teeth. The only thing left for him to do was to get back to the middle and see if he could get through La Escalera that way. But he had worn himself out, and it seemed to him that the water was going to enmesh him like a skein of a thousand threads. Young and strong as he was, those day had take a terrible toll. His brother, from the raft, made signs to him and shouted: "Make for the middle, the middle."

Rogelio finally made up his mind and let go of the projecting rock he was holding onto, and swam strongly through the current. He would like to cover leagues at each stroke, but he noticed that he was losing distance. Still he kept on swimming, followed by his brother's despairing eyes. Just a little more, and he would be in the middle . . . a little more. Yes, only a little more. Roge struggled on, defending his life and his hopes of love. It was a battle between effort and distance . . . Only a little more . . . But he was farther downstream . . . But he was going to reach the middle because if he didn't . . . His arms rose and fell in violent rhythm . . . Make for the middle, the middle . . . But the current was relentless: ten yards, five, two, one . . . The current had swallowed him up . . .

Arturo saw a black sphere which disappeared in the rush of water and an arm which stayed aloft a moment longer, as though bidding him farewell.

Then only the deafening roar of the waters breaking into foam. No trace whatever of his brother.

It seemed to him that an enormous buzzfly was circling about La Escalera. To his feverish ears the noise swelled and seemed to take on a low hum as of music. He was afraid he might be going mad and he threw himself face down on the raft, crawling over to the last gourd of rum, to press against it a long kiss from his dry, bitter lips. Finally he let it fall and the gourd rolled off into the water.

Arturo lay stretched out on the swaying raft, motionless and unconscious as a corpse. The sun cracked its merciless lash against his back.

8

Lay Aside Thy Anger, O Lord

Old Matías grew very difficult. Ever since the day he had hunted down the otter and had that presentiment, he was a different man. The worst of it was that when they looked at him Lucinda and Florinda began to whimper. Lucinda found consolation in her Adán, and the father of the other girl made her control her feelings. With a club in his hand he threatened to break her to bits if she kept on crying over that drunken, roving *cholo*. She dried her tears on her skirt and kept her woes to herself.

But the old man found no consolation, for Doña Melcha said never a word to him, fearful that he would send her to the devil if she tried to get his mind off his thoughts. Besides she, too, felt a shuddering fear in the depths of her heart. At the foot of the dense-foliaged mango tree which stood in front of his cabin, the old man lay down on a pile of deer skins and gave himself up to coca-chewing. A pile of dung burned beside him to keep the insects away and he lay there, a bundle of misery, his shirt unbuttoned and his belly bare. They had to carry his food outdoors to him and not even at night would he go inside the house.

"I don't know what ails me," he would sigh. "Oh my sons!"

The coca tasted as bitter as gall under his tongue and

this was the confirmation of his presage of misfortune.
He muttered oaths and kept repeating a blasphemous
prayer:

"Lay aside Thy anger, Thy justice, and Thy rigor,
And with Thy infinite patience—grind me in the
    dust, O Lord."

To be sure, these heretical challenges of Don Matías
had never prevented him from making his contribution
in money and rum toward the "devotion" of the Virgin.
In the days of her feast the priest came from Pataz,
traders from Celendín and people from all over. The
houses of Calemar were crowded with outsiders, and
what with prayers, processions and endless Lord's
Prayers for the souls of the dead, we got drunk as
surely as there is a God in Heaven. There was never
a lack of guitars, flutes, panpipes and drums, and by
day and by night the valley was a music box—*marineras, cashuas, huainos*—to which the river played the
accompaniment, and the trees and the wind.

The feast is a famous one, and why shouldn't it be
when the Virgin of Perpetual Help of Calemar, little as
she is and with such a small church, has more miracles
to her credit than the Virgin of Perpetual Help of Santiago, so big and with a fine church and candles burning
all year at the foot of her pedestal. Maybe it is because
our Virgin is a *gringa,* and the Lord likes her pink
cheeks and her blue eyes swimming in tears.

Anyway, the fact remained that old Matías had made
up his mind to die. I left him to himself, because it was
useless to try to do anything with him, and attended to
my work. "Let me alone, man, let me alone," he would
say. "Nobody's heart ever deceives him." So I went on
planting my bananas. I did not have to go to the mountains to get wood for ashes, for the flood had left plenty
of logs and brush on the bank. I made a pile and set it
afire. The red flames rose high in the sky and their heat
could be felt for many yards around. The logs were
still green, and sizzled as they burned, sweating fragrant

resins. Some tobacco plants near by were scorched. I rolled myself a cigarette and sat down on a rock by the river. As I watched the fire I could understand why there are people who set fires just for the fun of it. There is a wild fury in flames and they writhe and twist as though they would convert the whole earth into a live coal.

"Uaaa . . . Uaaa," came a faint cry. I went on watching the fire, but thinking how the grama grass had crept into the patch and would have to be cleaned out again. It would not be so hard this time, though.

"Uaaa . . . Uaaa," the cry kept on. I thought it was somebody driving the birds out of the banana groves farther down, but just to be on the safe side, I looked up the road. Nobody was coming down or going up. It must be . . .

"Uaaa . . . Uaaa," nearer now, upstream. I turned my head and saw the raft coming down. It was a big, good one that rode the water easily. In the prow sat a man all crumpled up who could barely move his paddle. What was this? Suddenly I recognized that it was Arturo, and I shouted at the top of my lungs, "Arturo-oo, Arturooo." My voice rang through the valley and old Matías was at my side in two strides. We understood one another without speaking a word, for he jumped in the water immediately and reached the raft just as it was drifting by.

Arturo looked at us, his face the color of suet and with the most vacant eyes I had ever seen. He threw us the paddle. "Take it," and fell back on the raft, unconscious. The old man dipped up water in his hands and threw it in his face. I began to row, and as we approached the bank I saw that there was nothing on the raft, only Arturo and the paddle. The poles were loose and looked as though they had been standing in the water.

We tied up at the bank and carried Arturo home on a litter. Lucinda's hands and feet were paralyzed by fright, and she stood there trembling like a sapling in a storm. Old Melcha from the gloomy frame of her doorway was the image of the Virgin of the Sorrows. Her eyes were mirrors of life which shivered into a thousand pieces. Florinda arrived in a few minutes. No words were necessary to bear out her fears, and she crouched in a corner mourning her misfortune.

A flock of parrots crossed overhead, wounding us with their raucous cries. We stretched Arturo out on blankets in a corner of the hut, and he fell asleep in the cool shade. The sound of the river invaded our silence with a harsh, grim mutter.

9

Arturo's Story

Arturo spent many days in bed. In the delirium of his fever he complained of the sun and shouted for Rogelio. Old Melcha rubbed him from head to foot with herbs and Don Matías forced his jaws open to make him swallow a little broth.

One day he sat up in bed looking around in all directions. His eyes rested on each of us as though he were seeing us for the first time in his life. At last he was back in the world and not in the hag-ridden pit of fever. At first he seemed to be counting the bamboo reeds of the wall, one by one. Yes, he really was in his house, here in Calemar, and there was Father Matías and Mamma Melcha, his wife Lucinda, and little Adán, and the *cholo* Lucas Vilca, too. Yes, he had been saved.

We squatted around him. Our eager expression made it look as though we were lying in wait for him. Finally he brought out his first faint words.

"Roge died."

We all knew it, but the confirmation chilled the soul of the old folks and their faces were drawn in tense, twitching lines of pain. Arturo went on hesitatingly, stopping to pull himself together, taking a swallow of water while great beads of perspiration broke out on his forehead.

When Roge was swallowed up by the river, Arturo fell over senseless on the raft. After that he didn't remember much. His last thought was to thrust his hands in the cracks between the poles of the raft. How long was he there, hours, days? Who can say? He felt a bump and the raft sort of straightened out, and inside his breast he heard a voice that was like his own say to him: "Save yourself." He managed to sit up, drawing strength from he knew not where and saw that the river had risen. The water came by very black, so he took hold of his paddle, throwing himself upon the mercy of the Virgin. The river was rising, the stench was terrible, and the raft made a movement as though it were shaking off its laziness and started to move forward. He rode along with the current and was swept right through the middle of La Escalera. The water roared like a maddened herd of cattle. The raft rushed past sharp rock points on one side and the other. Here was a whirlpool, there an outjutting rock in the middle of an eddy. Now they were rounding the curve with its projecting outcropping of stones. He tried to steer toward the other side, but a boatman is a poor thing at best, and besides there was no strength left in him. So the raft went headlong onto the cliff. Would the jolt tear it apart? "Virgin of Help, beautiful patroness," and he commended his soul into her hands. He raised his paddle toward the cliff to break the force of the blow. The impact almost knocked him off into the water, but it tempered the blow to the raft and it only came apart a little. The water held it against the cliff for a few seconds and then swung it to the right, in spite of his pushing with his paddle against the rock to get it back into the current. The curve made an eddy there and the raft began to spin around. He eyed the dreaded log jams longingly as they went by, hoping they would get him out of there, but the big logs went by on the opposite side where the current was strongest and only brush came into the whirlpool. And the raft kept whirling around until it reached the middle of the whirlpool, where it managed to keep from being sucked un-

der. It was big and new, and it sank only far enough for
the water to get his pants wet when the whirlpool
spewed it out again. It looked as though it were going
to get free but it banged against the cliff and started
whirling about all over again. "Virgin of Perpetual
Help, beautiful patroness," cried Arturo each time the
whirlpool seemed about to swallow him up. When he
was in the vortex, when he felt the creaking of the poles
as the roaring waters rushed over them, sometimes
covering him to the waist, in silence his whole life
passed before him.

Would he die like Roge? What about Mamma Melcha and Father Matías? The coca field would be green
now, green . . . and the peppers were just beginning to
turn. What made the water whistle that song he liked?
Poor Lucinda, she would never know what had happened. And little Adán, without a father. And poor old
Matías, so old now, would sigh for his sons when he
was no longer able to cross this flint-hearted river by
himself.

Raft, good stout raft! Now they were to one side
again. And once more they began spinning around.
"Here's where I am going to die," said Arturo. "It is
God's will, it is God's will." Until, finally, as the raft
made a broad turn, a huge, black log came along. It
passed to one side but he managed to reach it with the
paddle and steady himself against it. He held on hard,
hard. There was a moment of doubt in which it seemed
as though the log were going to follow them into the
whirlpool, but the current straightened it out full
length and it started downstream dragging them after it.
Now they were free. As the river comes out of the narrows it spreads out to its two broad banks, and he let
go the log. The sight of the banks was like life itself.
Stroke by stroke . . . He must save himself. But the raft
kept on down the middle without responding to his
feeble strokes. Until he saw the valley of Calemar . . .
His valley . . . And then he began to cry out.

"You all know what happened after that," Arturo
wound up his story.

"And where did you lose your poncho and the other things you were carrying in the water?" Lucinda inquired solicitously.

"Weren't they with me?" inquired Arturo in turn. In view of our thoughtful silence, he answered: "Then I don't know."

And he dropped back on his many-colored blankets. Old Melcha wept and Don Matías, huddled up and silent, looked like a stone idol. Arturo fell into a deep sleep and I watched him with admiring eyes.

"There's a brave *cholo*," I said to Don Matías.

The old man turned toward me, fixing me with a look that came from centuries past.

"So is the river. Trying to get the better of it means death for us sometimes. But we don't flee from it because we are men and we have to take things as they come."

10

Fiesta

In our part of the country life takes on many aspects and meanings: it can wound, give and take, throw up floods of suffering and dig channels of death and desolation. It can blow gales of hatred and shoot out deadly flashes of lightning, ripen the fruit, and bring love into flower. It can make one sing and also weep, but once a year, for a fortnight, it assumes a single expression. All destinies come together in a wild union: the fiesta.

And fiesta-time had arrived.

Calemar overflowed with visitors and rejoicing. Natives and visitors all had new clothes for the occasion, displaying against the intense green of trees and plants a rainbow of bright colors. People traded, ate, drank, and danced. It was a period of unalloyed happiness.

Besides, the priest came to say mass for the Blessed Virgin and the souls of the departed. Don Casimiro Baltodano, the parish priest of Pataz, had come, like every other year, for he was always asked by reason of the qualities that made him a fine priest: with his deep resonant voice he officiated at the high mass sung on the most important day of the festival, and he never refused to go through the measures of the dance or take a drink.

All the merrymakers showered him with attentions

and on the day of his arrival he was received with music and fireworks, not to mention the drinks.

"Long live *taita* priest!"

"Long may he live."

The priest came into town on his weather-beaten old brown mule, which was not frightened by the noise or the crowding around of the *cholos,* nor the screeching of the flute or the booming of the drums, and even less by the explosion of the firecrackers. Every now and then he pulled up the mule to try a gourd of *chicha* or a half glass of rum. At times he passed a little of the drink on to the sexton, a timid-looking *cholo* who came riding behind him on a bony nag.

"Long live *taita* priest."

"Long may he live."

Yesterday he officiated at a mass in honor of the Virgin and celebrated ten marriages and twenty baptisms. He chanted very well, for you could hear him a long way from the church and the sexton swung the censer of incense about making a thick smoke and everybody was happy.

Today he also said a high mass for the dead in the family of Don Juan Plaza, as he does every year, and he finished marrying all the engaged couples and baptizing all those as yet unsanctified. Tomorrow he would begin his masses for the repose of the souls of departed relatives of the villagers. In the meantime the priest visited around, eating and drinking of the finest and dancing with the prettiest girls he could find.

"Long live *taita* priest!"

"Long may he live."

Besides Don Juan Plaza many others came, as was to be expected. What a crowd of people! Indians from Bambamarca and Condormarca, and, from the other side, the never-failing merchants from Celendín—barefooted but with a full pocket—and even a rancher who had brought a string of mules and muleteers to take back coca.

The cabins were crowded, not only with people, but with the products the people from the valley and their visitors exchanged, which were piled up in baskets on the porches. Many houses displayed banners, flapping lazily in the wind, which advertised the different articles they had for sale: the red ones announced *chicha;* the green ones, coca; the blue ones, sugar cane syrup and rum; the white ones, bread. The traders from Celendín spread out in the patios their packs of merchandise: bright-colored percales, shiny mirrors and knives, white hats. Not a thing was missing.

And over this way there was the sound of guitars, and that way of drums, and here, *marineras,* and there, *cashuas.*

In the evening, after eating, the dancing stopped for a moment. The sky which was just lighting its early stars saw us all, valley folk and visitors, go to church.

The Blessed Virgin of Perpetual Help of Calemar stood at the back in the center of an altar covered with candles which rose row upon row from the floor to the ceiling and burned with a palpitating red flicker. They gave forth an odor of suet which mingled with that of the incense the devout were burning. The little miracle-working image wore a bright silk cloak, embroidered in gold, and her face was tilted Heavenward. Her eyes were blue, her cheeks rosy, and her mouth a deep red. One of her hands was lost from view among the pleated folds of her robe, and the other, pink, delicate and generous, reached out to bless the worshipping *cholos* crowded about her feet.

What is there that lovely face could not obtain! To her the prayers for one's own soul and those of the dead are directed. The supplicant, kneeling at the feet of the image, said the first part of the Lord's Prayer and the group chanted the rest. The voices came together and blended in a solemn, plaintive, monotonous music.

"A little prayer for the soul of the late Pedro Ruiz."

The mournful prayer sounded like a lament.

"A little prayer for the soul of the late Martín Blas."

As many prayers as there were dead. This time the name of Roge was among the list. "Forgive us our tres-

passes as we forgive those who trespass . . . Lead us
not into temptation . . . from evil . . . Amen."

From the huddled mass of heads, shawls and
ponchos, which covered the floor before the altar so
thickly that not the least bit of bare space was visible,
the prayers ascended, forming, with the incense, a cloud
that rose toward the Virgin, that rose toward God,
paying them homage and pleading that the souls of the
living be forgiven and those of the dead, saved.

Then came the dance again.

In the darkness of the night, when the wind swayed
the trees in the midst of the music which filled the
valley, they seemed to be dancing, too. The river as it
flowed by gave a great deal of happy laughter and the
echoes that followed our shouts of rejoicing might have
been the voices of the crags that shared in our delight.

From the house furtive couples, the newly married
or those for whom the sacrament had not yet been said,
slipped away. Watching cautiously for snakes, they
took each other on a bed of earth, feverish with drink
and desire, beneath the cover of the darkness glittering
with stars, possessed by the fire which kindled body and
soul in the torrid nights of the Marañón.

The one who suffered and yet rejoiced in the midst
of his many obligations and the exercise of his power
was Florencio Obando. As in other years, by his authority as Lieutenant Governor, he had prepared for the
festival, appointing two of the strongest *cholos* in the
valley as his deputies. If anybody started throwing his
weight around, one of the deputies stretched him out,
and when he awoke he was a model of good behavior.

Florencio Obando enjoyed the widest authority and
respect. Years before, after a number of changes, he
had been elected Lieutenant Governor by acclamation
of the whole valley, and in the face of such a unani-
mous vote, his appointments had been officially recognized. The proper authorities turned over to him the
seal and badge of office. He had made very little use of
them ever since he received them and that is why we
were all so pleased with him.

To put it in a word, he knew how to do things. Presents of chickens or rum carried no weight with him when it came to imprisoning or freeing anybody. Neither did he send prisoners to the capital of the province. In his opinion, locking them up in the church—when there were no worshippers, naturally—was enough, as it should be. He was the one who decided that Martín had given Pablo grounds for provocation in the matter of the balsa tree, and that was the end of the affair. And he was the one who told the troopers that the Romeros no longer lived there when they came looking for them. All this won him the esteem of everybody, but his reputation increased and spread as the result of a *marinera* couplet which he himself composed:

> I am the first,
> I am the second,
> I am the Lieutenant Governor.

He was well along in years—at least fifty—and, as can be seen, he was a man of good sense. And what added even more to the high regard in which he was held was the fact that he did all this without knowing how to read or write. When he had to draw up a document for his immediate superior, the Governor of Bambamarca, attenuating the faults charged against the valley people, or explaining his inability to apprehend somebody, it was his son who did the writing. But Obando, either to enhance the solemnity of the act, or to show that he completely agreed with the facts set forth therein, stamped his seal on the four corners of the paper.

Now Florencio Obando went back and forth, followed by his deputies, to make sure that the merchants from Celendín were not robbed, settling disputes, calming down quarrels, without any of these activities preventing him from having an occasional swallow.

Since the church was open for worship day and night, and could not be used as a jail, severe measures were more than ever necessary. If anybody failed to show him proper respect or attempted to overstep bounds, his deputies were on hand to make him understand how great was the power of Florencio Obando, the Lieutenant Governor of the Village of Calemar.

The third mass was held that morning, the first of those to be said in the next day or so for the souls of the departed. Though we reeked of stews, coca and rum, and our faces were haggard from not sleeping enough, we all listened to it devoutly. May the souls for whom it was said be saved and enjoy eternal peace!

But a few hours later the people began to grumble because word leaked out that the priest had not used wine for the Consecration but a mixture of rum and ale, for the night before he had drunk up the wine he had brought with him in the spree he went on with Don Juan Plaza.

Suspicion spread, and a fellow from Bambamarca went to him and asked when he was going to say the mass that he had arranged for.

"I said it this morning, my son," was the answer.

And then people from the valley and the highlands went with the same question, and to all he made the same answer: "I said it this morning, my son."

All commentary was superfluous. A discussion began about the purpose of the mass; amazement and indignation grew until finally a committee was named to lay a protest.

The priest was standing at the end of the porch before the house of Manuel Campos, where he was staying—Campos was an old friend of his from Pataz. He listened gravely to the complaints of the commission, with cheeks puffed out and eyebrows raised.

When they had finished, he condescended to explain matters, and raising his arms Heavenward from time to time, he said: "It is the intention that counts, my children. . . . The same mass may be said for many souls at the same time. What we ask for is everlasting rest in the arms of Our Lord, and it is the same to pray for many as to pray for one at the same mass. All this is in keeping with the laws of the Holy Church which is ruled over by the Holy Father in Rome who is the representative of Our Father which art in Heaven. . . ."

A few voices could be heard above the murmur of dissatisfaction: "But *taita* priest, last year it wasn't this way. You said a mass for every person who paid you to say it. Look how yesterday you said one just for Don Juan Plaza. . . . That has always been the way."

Don Casimiro Baltodano crossed his arms, stuck out his stomach still farther as he rocked back on his heels, and answered in an overbearing tone: "It's the custom, but it's a mistake. If you want a special mass, just because you feel like it, it will cost you five *soles* each."

The women in the commission begged plaintively: "But *taita* priest, don't be that way. . . . Think of the poor souls. . . ."

"What will God say to you on Judgment Day?"

The priest maintained his overbearing attitude, and adduced a new argument to justify his fee: "If you want a special mass, it will cost you five *soles* each. Why, two *soles* doesn't even pay for the wine."

At this point a wave of indignation rose in the breasts of all present, and sharp words showered down upon him.

"What a liar!"

"He used rum and ale to consecrate."

"What impudence!"

"That's what he is, impudent."

Seeing that his authority was undermined, the priest decided on an orderly retreat, raising both arms and eyes Heavenward.

"I am not deceiving you. . . . As God is my witness!"

And with a few long, swift strides he gained the inside of the house. The commission went away, talking about the priest with frequent references to the Devil, and broke up as its various members came to the road each had to take.

The news spread quickly through the whole valley and then nobody felt like dancing. People drank, as they will, to kill the bad time they were going through.

The men at the doors of their houses, under the trees, leaning over the fences, gathered along the roads, emptied gourds of liquor, and voiced their indignation. The women, as they prepared their meals, or washed the jugs along the flume, kept right up with the men in their tongue-wagging.

"The priest has become a miser."

"Who ever heard of such a lack of consideration toward a soul. . . ."

"And, above all, by a priest."

"He's damned, he'll never see the face of God."

The *cholos* reviewed every detail. It was not so bad to be a drunkard, but it was unpardonable to have drunk up the consecrated wine, as well as to have said only one mass for the dead and to have charged for twenty. Then they pointed out that the priest ate, drank and grew fat at the expense of the poor, and why? It's not very hard work going about in a cassock and saying things that nobody understands in front of the same book all the time. Even the sexton came in for the most withering comments.

"What does that one do? He doesn't even answer so you can hear him at mass."

"He doesn't even move the censer."

"You said it. All those who are too lazy to work become sextons."

"Skirt-wearers like women, like the priests themselves."

"If he's a man let him work the land."

"Let him get himself a yoke of oxen."

After all was said and done, what could they do? The priest found smooth words to justify himself. And so when night came, they ate and drank and began to dance again. And *marineras, cashuas* and *chiquitas* once more made legs and hips come to life. And breasts quivered and eyes gleamed.

"Hooray for the fiesta!"

"Down with the thieving priest."

And between shout and shout, verses began to spread. *Marineras* and *chiquitas,* whose words expressed the protest and the slyness of the valley people, became audible. All Calemar was a wide smile which showed sharp *cholo* teeth.

> "Ay, Maria Rosa,
>   What have you been up to,
>   Out in the dark night
>   With the reverend father?"

"Ha-ha," burst out the mirth of singers and dancers. "Let's have another one of those songs that tells the truth."

> "I had a girl,
>   Her name was Dionisia.
>   The priest took her from me
>   Saying she was the first fruit."

And it was adding fuel to the fire when the news began to spread that the priest was leaving the next day. Of course, if he had no more masses to say he'd have to leave and the most astonishing thing was that they hadn't realized it. So the priest was actually planning to leave! This was really getting intolerable.

It was at a dance where there were only valley people that the matter assumed really serious proportions because the honor of Calemar was involved. An old wrinkled woman was almost beside herself.

"The man has no conscience, seems like. All my life I've lived here in Calemar, and I never before saw a priest behave this way. . . ."

She trembled from head to foot. Her hair came down. Standing there in the middle of the cabin, her eyes veered from one *cholo* to another. The yellowish candle that barely lighted up the room made her face look still paler.

"But the reason is because the men stand for it. They don't seem like people from the valley any more, they're so lily-livered."

A stab in the back could not have aroused greater

wrath in Venancio Landauro. Pushing his hat back from his forehead and spitting out his wad of coca as is the custom when a fight is in the making, he gave a bang on the table and growled: "I am going to stop him before he gets away . . . anyone who wants to come along with me is welcome."

Landauro was from Shicún. Of course Calemar could do no less. In a minute a dozen *cholos* were at his side.

"Let's go."

Then Venancio added: "And if he doesn't want to stay, we'll have to give him a beating. Once when I was in Marcabalito I saw them give the priest a first-class beating. I took a couple of pokes at him myself."

"That's what those rascally priests need."

"We'll teach him that he can't fool around with Cale-mar."

And they went out shouting and brandishing their fists. Behind them followed the women carrying sticks and stones. One who had kept his head through the excitement stopped the group.

"First we should go and see the Lieutenant Governor."

"That's right, let Florencio tell him to say the masses or give us back our money."

Florencio Obando was at home when they arrived there a minute later, and he did not require any coaxing for he, too, had paid for a mass. Accompanied by his deputies, with whom he had been having supper, he joined the group.

"We have to cut off his escape or make him return the money," agreed Florencio.

"Hooray for the Lieutenant Governor."

"Hooraaay."

All the merrymakers rushed to see what had happened and the group grew with those who joined the cause. The valley echoed with the shouts.

"Down with the thieving priest."

"Dooown with him."

They finally reached the priest's lodging. The *cholos* were swaying and threatening, drunk and angry.

"Let the priest come out."

"Send him out."

Manuel Campos came to the door looking all around to see if there was any possibility of escape, but the group of *cholos* had surrounded the cabin. The darkness of the house had aroused their suspicions, for not even a candle was burning there in spite of the fact that the shadows of the starry night had become black darkness inside the house.

"It's not you we want, it's the priest."

"Tell him to come out."

The master of the house answered in a quavering voice: "He's not here."

"Let him come out peaceable so we can settle this matter without trouble."

A clenched fist was brandished under the *cholo* Campos's nose. The tumult grew by the minute.

A woman's voice screeched: "And the sexton, too."

"Let the skirt-wearer come out, too, let him come out," insisted many voices.

At that moment the sexton made his appearance, cringing, as though he were about to break in two. He was a skinny, sickly looking half-breed. He tried to explain matters, and gestured, but his voice broke and his arms trembled. Clasping his hands together he pleaded rather than affirmed: "He isn't here, he left a while ago?"

"And where did he go?" demanded the Lieutenant Governor.

"Make him tell . . . make him tell."

The voices of the women egged the crowd on. The voices of the *cholos* were menacing.

"I can't, I don't know where he went," he insisted.

A stone whistled past his head. The *cholo* Campos managed in some way to break through the crowd and make for the woods. Florencio Obando felt that the moment had come for him to assert his authority and

with one slap he laid the trembling servant of the priest
out on the ground.

"You liar!"

The sexton writhed as a mass of feet kicked at him.
When he tried to get up a shower of blows laid him low
again.

"Where am I? Don't hit me any more, I'm a sick
man," he pleaded, howling with pain.

"Sick, are you? That's what makes you such a good
liar, I suppose."

"Let him have it, good and plenty."

There came a moment when his body lay motionless
and the voice ceased its clamor, and the group moved
away to take counsel.

"He's in the woods, I'll bet."

"Let's go after him."

Suddenly the sound of galloping hoofs came to them
and a voice cried out: "There he goes. . . . That's the
priest over that way."

In the midst of the darkness and the forest the click
of fleeing hoofbeats was barely audible. They disappeared. They were going uphill.

When they started making inquiries a woman told
them: "He went past my house and he was riding
bareback."

Some of the *cholos,* with Florencio Obando at their
head, mounted bareback, too, and set out like the wind
toward the road. The alert listeners could hear the noise
of the race. The light hoofbeats they had first heard
were now drowned out. Finally the rush of the four
horses carrying the pursuers died down, too, in the distance. Then shots were heard and in a little while the
cholos returned and explained that the priest had
stopped and fired at them and for that reason they
couldn't get near him.

"Down with that thieving priest."

"Down with him."

"Hooray for the Lieutenant Governor."

"Hooray."

After a number of drinks the dance began again. The

music spread its merry notes throughout the valley. Meanwhile beside a ditch where he had managed to drag his battered body, the sexton washed his wounds in silence.

Now that the priest and other scamps had left town—the sexton made off on the third day—we could still have a good time, for the souls of the departed would forgive us for not saying masses for them as it wasn't our fault.

It was good to be alive. We ate, we drank, we danced and we made love in simple and homely fashion. Life was wonderfully good.

"Here's to your good health."

"Until the next one in honor of the Virgin."

"That's right, to the Virgin."

Fiesta, the gay fiesta of every year. Voices were raised in song, flutes shrilled, drums bellowed, panpipes sobbed, guitars trilled. Our privations and our achievements, our disappointments and our hopes, our griefs and our joys were all intermingled in a single sense of well-being made up of drunkenness and dance.

11

Home Thoughts

At first only sun showers fell, but then the skies became thickly overcast, clouds took on the color of lead and rusty iron, until they finally burst in a downfall of water, thunder and lightning.

And there was the rainy season again. It had come upon us all of a sudden.

The cabins shook, the hills shuddered, the river swelled, and from the waterlogged earth, humid and spongy, the thick grass sprang and the trees put on a new green.

When the sun managed to show itself through a rare fragment of clear sky, the washed crags looked redder than ever, the trees glistened like new, and the river—black with mud, convulsed with log jams—was a dark brush stroke against the gay many-colored background of nature. But the sun stayed out only a short while, and the canyon was always gray, as though it were full of ashes and the sky hung overhead like a threat.

The rain fell day and night, and sometimes in the morning, as well, so we had to stay in our huts. We pulled our rafts back a good distance from the riverbank so they would not be swept away by the rising current. We closed the intake of the sluices so that the brook's swollen stream would not flood the valley.

And we settled down to our coca, and our talk, unless it occurred to some witless soul to want to cross the river.

It rained and rained. The river rumbled and the rain pattered noisily on the leaves. A stiff gust of wind shook the trees, making streams of water pour off them, and drove some of the storm through the reed walls. The canyon was a whistling, roaring pocket.

During the moments of calm the shrill chirping of the crickets became audible as did the hooting of the owls which had taken refuge in the crevices of the crags. The other birds fluttered heavily from tree to tree without finding rest for the soles of their feet. They would have to migrate God only knows where or die. How and where do birds end their days? Those which manage to escape their enemies—man and beast —why and when do they die?

We were discussing this matter in Don Matías's cabin. I had been there ever since the morning when I took a group of folks from Bambamarca across the river. Silverio Cruz had come from his place to get fire and he had not gone yet. Talking on and on time had slipped by and the rain had begun again, and he was afraid it might put out his embers even though he kept the clay pan covered with his poncho.

"Yes, sir," said Don Matías, "one thing I'd like to know is how the birds die. I've never found one dead in the fields unless a snake or some other animal had killed it and left only the feathers or it had been shot, but you can always tell that. But one that died a natural death, never."

Old Melcha, who was sitting in a corner with Lucinda winding into balls the skeins of wool which they had traded for coca with the Indians from the highlands, observed: "Those are matters for God, man. Who can know that? Only He . . ."

"Only He," repeated Lucinda, deftly moving the ball on which she was winding the gray yarn from the skein Doña Melcha held tightly across her hands.

Adán, sitting beside his father, listened attentively

without understanding what it was all about. Arturo believed in the virtues of education, and said, although the matter did not interest him much: "I think those educated gentlemen in the cities are the ones who know."

At this point Don Matías interrupted him, raising his voice, not only to emphasize his point, but because the roaring of the river was getting louder, making it difficult to hear: "Oh yes, they say they know, but it's not the same to know that a thing is true as to have seen it with your own eyes."

Silverio Cruz, who had been waiting for an opportune moment, broke in to ask them to listen to him.

"This damned storm . . . while it clears up I'm going to tell you how the birds die. Listen to me. . . ."

"Go ahead, man, go ahead."

"When I was a boy my mamma used to tell a story that she had heard when she was a girl. They say that a man went out to cut some wood. He couldn't seem to find any so he kept on walking along a ravine. He was going through the brush, and there was no good wood anywhere, nothing but green saplings. So he kept going on when all of a sudden he heard birds singing. He came up softly and he said that he saw a big field where the birds had gathered and were sitting in the branches all around the opening. There were all kinds of birds, red, green, brown, yellow, some called *huanchacos,* others *chiscos, rocoteros, quiénquiénes* . . . and other birds he had never seen before in his life, never. And they were sitting there singing, and the man stood there, enchanted, listening to their song, for they all sang together and it was the most beautiful song a Christian ever heard. When all of a sudden the birds stopped singing, and one of them who was on the tip-top branch and who looked pretty old, for his plumage had no gloss on it, suddenly began to fly up, higher and higher, circling round and round till the man could no longer see him, nor the other birds, either, for he flew into the clouds, above the clouds, right into Heaven."

"Go on, man, go on, but that isn't dying," remarked the old man, in amazement.

"But that's the death of a bird," went on Silverio, "for a bird goes right to heaven without the least harm to his body."

"Do you mean it, man?"

The narrator was carried away by his story and the general admiration he had awakened. Even the women were looking at him with wide-eyed amazement, and he went on.

"Well now . . . Just then the birds noticed the man, and one of them flew over to a branch near by and spoke to him just like he was another man, and said these words to him: 'You have seen what no human being has ever seen. If you tell it, you will die.' Then the man promised never to say a word, and he kept his word because he knew that if he did not do it he would die."

"Well, well," commented Don Matías, "that must be the way it happens, for how else could you explain that we have never found a bird dead of a natural death?"

Silverio Cruz blew into the clay dish to quicken the red glow of the embers. Then he put it down to one side, smiled and shook his lime gourd and chewed his coca with an air of satisfaction.

But Arturo was in an argumentative mood, and at no pains to conceal it.

"Yes, but see here, if the man couldn't tell and didn't, as you say, how was it ever found out?"

As the others watched him reflectively, he added: "It's just a story someone has made up."

"That might be, too," added the old man, after a moment's thought.

The visitor was caught somewhat off balance, but he tried to defend himself: "Who knows but what he told it in a dream, and then it wasn't his fault?"

His listeners laughed ironically.

"Oh, no, who ever heard of anybody telling a story as long as that in a dream."

Even Adán smiled showing the shining little teeth in his small round dark face. The storyteller accepted the objection but not with too good a grace.

"Well, that may be the case, but that's the way my mamma told it. . . ."

And then he said good-bye. He had to leave before the darkness and the rain got heavier.

"Has the brook risen much?"

Silverio Cruz who saw it every day because his cabin and his fields were alongside it, answered firmly: "No, it hasn't risen what you would call much. And now even if it should rise it wouldn't matter, for the bed is very deep and it won't overflow."

With the pot of embers under his poncho he stepped out into the rain, which ran trickling down his back, and he was soon lost from sight among the trees.

A moment later there was a terrific clap of thunder, the water began to come down in sheets and the wind started howling. The old man listened anxiously to the rising fury of the storm.

"I hope the brook isn't going to overflow. There's a lot of underbrush falling. You hear those dogs?"

All through the other houses of the valley the dogs were barking and howling distressfully.

12

The Uta and the Blue Puma

Doña Mariana Chiguala was an old woman. She always dressed in coarse black woolen clothes, she lived at the foot of the valley, near Encarna's house, and hers was a sad story. She told it to whoever went to see her with many details, and tears which she brushed away with the back of her hand; how it was that she lost her husband who, many years before, went to Huamachuco, to sell some coca, and was drafted into the army and never returned.

"Perhaps he has died," she would exclaim, bursting into sobs.

Then she would tell how she lived with her niece, Hormecinda, whose parents wanted her to raise the girl. And, as it began to get dark, we would see Hormecinda, bashful and red-cheeked, come driving her herd of goats.

If the person to whom Doña Mariana was talking listened to her with attention, she would tell all the incidents that preceded her marriage (for she had gone straight from her house to the church—thank God—without first having lived in sin the way some did) and then she would sing the praises of her husband, who had been a great coca gatherer and the best boatman, and had possessed all the virtues of a good Christian.

Finally, if the listener was softhearted, she would

open her heart and sigh about the lonely life she led, for her niece Hormecinda was young and hadn't much sense yet.

Folks said that Encarna visited her at times, unbeknownst to his wife, but that was really just gossip. What was a fact though was that any stranger who took lodging at her house stayed there three days. There was a man from Celendín by the name of Abdón who always went there when he came through. He was the one who would know.

The fact was that I had to deal with Doña Mariana about my meals. When my parents died I tried to cook for myself, but it was a nuisance and it took a lot of time. Besides, I burned the yuccas and burned the pots. After I had broken three, I went to see the lady. She has been cooking for me ever since, and going into my garden as though it were her own to get yuccas, chile, bananas—whatever was there. She was kind of tempting, too. She wasn't ugly; she was well built, with full lips, and hips and bosom still firm and solid. The *cholos* always would say to me: "Go ahead, man, what are you waiting for?"

But I did not say one word out of line to her, for, if a man from the valley wants a little fun, let him find it somewhere else, or else he'll never get free. No, not yet. Nobody but me knew that it was Florinda I wanted to talk with, but she always kept her eyes on the ground and wouldn't even look at the *cholos*.

Now, when I went in to lunch, Doña Mariana kept up a steady stream of conversation while she filled my gourds.

"You must have spent a bad night with the storm."

"Yes, but it's nothing new and you get used to it."

And then, she went on in search of further details: "As still as it is around your place, aren't you afraid of snakes biting you? Do you light a candle?"

"When I think about it, I do."

"Goodness gracious . . . you must always light a candle."

A fine misty rain began to fall.

Then she told me that she had been very much afraid, for the puma had come, taking advantage of the dark stormy night, and had been prowling around her place. It may even have been trying to get into the fold. The goats were bleating fearsomely and the dog, Matarrayo, barked in terror and refused to step outside the door though she and Hormecinda kept sicking him on.

Just then the three peals of a bell sounded which was Arturo's way of calling the men of his group. Arturo was now chief boatman, for Don Matías was not feeling well. So I said good-bye to Doña Mariana and went by my house first to get my paddle.

"There are two fellows coming down over that way," said Arturo as soon as I came up. "As it's early they'll probably want to be carried across."

The *cholos* Jacinto Huamán and Santos Ruiz, who had taken Roge's place, were already with him. While we were waiting we looked our paddles over to make sure that the handles weren't loose. Old Matías came out on the porch grumbling and complaining about the weather. His joints ached and, when it rained, it was impossible for him to row.

"Damn fools. Not even a cloudburst will stop them running back and forth so you have to ferry them across," he growled, angrily shaking his lime gourd.

We sat down beside the door and it wasn't long before two Christians, who certainly did not look the part, came up. They greeted us in hoarse voices, shook the water off their ponchos at the edge of the porch, and then asked for lodgings.

"Will you let us spend the night here, Don Matías, and tomorrow we'll go across?"

"Of course, of course, come in," answered the old man, granting them the hospitality that he never refused.

"May God repay you, sir."

Arturo, seeing that they were looking at our paddles, remarked: "We thought you'd be wanting to cross right away. . . ."

"We would have crossed . . . but we're in such a bad fix . . . and traveling with this rain. . . ."

As a matter of fact, they did not have to justify their delay. Their swollen faces were pitiful to behold, the movements of their bodies were heavy and lifeless, and their voices were a wail of suffering. They were *utosos;* they had caught *uta,* an illness characteristic of the Marañón valleys, but which takes its greatest toll among those who do not live there, but are there only temporarily. First somewhere on the body a red spot appears which turns purplish and then bursts, forming a running sore full of pus. Then sores break out all over the body and the flesh slowly rots. A man becomes a piece of carrion.

The *utosos* sat down at one end of the porch and looked out upon the rain with sad, dull eyes, eyes bereft of all hope. A brief light came into them as they answered to Don Matías question.

"We're from Condormarca. . . . We're going to Huamachuco where they say the doctor can cure us. . . ."

Their faces were purple and their features had disappeared, leaving just two slabs of flesh. They were so swollen that it seemed that trickles of blood were going to burst from them, but what happened was that they broke out in eruptions and running sores along the jaw. The nose of one had been eaten away leaving nothing but a dark hole, and one side of the other's had already rotted away.

Don Matías sympathized with their illness, which should be treated very early if it is to be cured, and asked them if they had ever tried "soldier's salve." They replied in the negative and went on to say that all they used was plantain leaves, and butter made from woman's milk and other things the healer of their town had recommended.

Don Matías said: "My friend Roque, who is dead, got the *uta* and he used that remedy and he got well."

Then he went on: "I can't figure out why the devil it is. As long as I have lived in Calemar, which is my whole life, I have seen only two valley people get *uta*, and I am sick of seeing folks from other places, especially the highlands, get it right off. I wonder why it is. I can't understand it."

"It's God's will," muttered the two victims, almost in the same breath and with the same sad voice. They looked out upon the trees of the steaming, fertile valley with grief and wrath. Something hidden and tragic rose up in their stricken eyes. If only the valley were like the highlands, free from all evil. But here, hidden in this overpowering, lush vegetation, there was a plant which, when bitten by a mosquito who then bites a person, produces this sickness.

Jacinto and Santos were going home the next morning and I was going to go, too, but Don Matías' valley cordiality kept me there.

"Come on, waif, why do you want to get wet going and coming from your house to Doña Mariana's and then here. . . . It will be better for you to stay here."

Night closed in and the guests, the same as we, drew up to the fireplace where the pots were steaming. One of them was so advanced in his illness that his hands were puffed up like those of a corpse. They could barely drink their soup through their thickened, raw lips. When they chewed it seemed as though their trembling cheeks were going to split and fall in the gourd dishes or to the floor. And there was a bad smell about them, the smell of the tomb.

"May God repay you, sir," they said gratefully when they finished eating.

Arturo tried to cheer them up.

"Don't worry, you'll get all right. I've seen people who had *uta* get well, over at Sartín. Early tomorrow morning we'll take you across so you can get there as soon as possible."

He left them, accompanied by Lucinda and Adán, and they ran toward their own cabin. The old man and Doña Melcha got into their little room and we settled ourselves on the porch, they at one end and I in the bunk that used to be Roge's.

Night closed heavily in on the cabin, and it was impossible to see a thing, but I could feel close by the sad, tragic company of these two men with their illness that presaged the tomb, that was already a living death. The rain fell heavily upon the silence which was both sleep and death. Suddenly life still made itself felt in one of them. In a low, muted voice which could not restrain its profound sorrow he said:

"I feel awful bad . . . it hurts me inside . . . the sickness is reaching my heart, I am sure."

And in the morning, after we had eaten, we started toward the river, the *utosos* following us. They walked behind us with short, slow steps, avoiding every brusque movement as if they were afraid their flesh were going to come apart and fall off them.

"It rained all night and the river must be pretty high."

"I'll bet it is, too."

With our paddles over our shoulders we proceeded down the street. Heavy drops were still dripping from the trees. And a mist that felt wet against our skins rose, enveloping Calemar as though the whole valley were boiling like a big pot. Slowly, slowly the thin pale clouds rose to thicken in the sky and then, in the afternoon, fell in a furious storm.

We came to the river, tempestuous and black, and roaring menace at us. Through the curtain of mist, the other bank was barely visible. Now we had to push the raft down. The *utosos* wanted to help us, but Arturo gently prevented them.

"Don't you bother. . . . What you men need is lots of rest."

And the raft slipped down the smooth runway of *sinamomo* and orangewood planks that was built for this purpose and into the water where it began to ride and pull on the rope by which Jacinto was holding it. As the waves heaved it violently up and down, it seemed very frail and as if the river could easily drag it away. But that was reckoning without us, the boatmen of Calemar. And without our paddles and our arms.

Arturo leaped into the middle of the raft and began swaying his body from one side to the other to steady its balance. The rushing water was black with mud. The banks were completely submerged and not a stone was to be seen.

"Logs, logs," shouted Santos suddenly.

There were some logs floating down the middle of the river which could have been the presage of a jam. Our head boatman stayed in the raft, but, at his orders, we waited on the bank. Without paying any attention to the muddy wet soil, the *utosos* sat down and began to talk in low voices.

In the distance, dimly through the mist, we managed to make out a jam which darkened as it approached and became an enormous, tangled mass, against which we realized that all resistance would have been useless. It would have caught us in the middle of the river. Rocking heavily along with the rise and fall of the waves, the mass of logs and brush floated by, stretching almost from one bank to the other. The top of an enormous *gualango* trunk, still fresh and green, hit the raft and gave it a sharp push. There were heavy trees of which only the branches were visible.

When the last vestiges of the jam had disappeared far below, Arturo broke the silence.

"Now to the raft, men, let's get over fast; come on, fellows."

We jumped aboard but the *utosos* did not follow us. One of them was stretched full length on the ground. The other kept his eyes fixed on him, and did not turn his head when Jacinto, who was waiting for them to get on in order to follow them, for he was still on the ground holding back the raft with the rope, said: "Come on, men, we've got to get across fast."

The one who was stretched out raised himself slowly on his elbows and said in a hoarse, suffering voice: "What's the use, now? The sickness has reached my heart already."

And then he fell as though he had been knocked

over by a crushing blow, his face sinking into the muddy earth. The other turned him over, taking him gently by the shoulder. The ulcerous face was covered with mud. With swollen, trembling forefinger his companion tried to push up one of the swollen eyelids. The eye was staring and sightless.

The Indian sat there motionless. What a storm of desolation and horror must have broken in his soul! But his featureless face, swollen and covered with purplish ulcers, gave no sign. Only his voice reflected his utter affliction, as he turned to us and said: "Help me to bury him, Christians. Do me this favor."

The body was laid out on the porch of old Matías's house, on a bed of banana leaves and *yerbasanta*. A rope fastened the blankets in which he was swathed, going around and around from his head to his feet in many tight windings. His face was hidden under a sheepskin.

This is how the dead are buried in our part of the country, if they have died where there are kind-hearted Christians. The purpose of the rope is not merely to fasten the blankets. Its main object is to keep the soul from escaping from the imprisoned body to wander over the earth in torment. It must leave by the head— that is why the sheepskin is not pulled up over the crown of the head—and go straight before God to be judged.

Doña Melcha and the women of the valley who had come to the wake were at work hulling wheat that had been soaking in lye. The men came bringing coca, sugar-cane syrup and rum, and they sat down one by one on the edge of the porch. They talked in low voices chewing their coca and drinking when they were not eating from the gourd plates which were passed around full of yucca, stewed corn and dried meat. And they listened to the other *utoso* who, seated beside the fetid, swathed corpse, and driving away with a banana leaf the swarm of flies that hovered about the living and the dead, said: "Poor Damián, he never deserved such a death as this."

After a moment's silence he went on: "He was a good man, he was, and to die like this! Because it's always sad to die far away from home, even though there are good people who take pity on you and give you a decent burial. . . ."

"That's true, that certainly is the truth," answered the *cholos* closest to him.

The *utoso* went on in his sad, slow voice: "And a good worker he was, too. Sick and all as he was he left a patch of potatoes all ready to be hilled up and a field of barley that was just about ready to cut. . . ."

Then he fell into a deep silence just moving his hands to shake the banana leaf and keep away the persistent buzzing flies. When some new arrival asked him a question he always answered the same way: "He didn't deserve a death like this."

And he kept on about how sad it was to die far from one's own home, no matter how kind people were and even if they gave you a decent burial.

If he forgot to mention what a worker he had been, the *cholos* added the details: "He left a patch of potatoes. . . ."

"And a field of ripe barley, too."

"God rest his soul, poor fellow."

In the afternoon the heat grew more intense and the corpse began to give off a nauseating smell. The stench was so great it was impossible to breathe comfortably in the room, even though the wind blew through it all the time. Even the clothes of the living reeked with the fetid smell, and the *cholos,* to drown it out, kept drinking generous measures of rum. By nightfall all the liquor was gone, and then the *utoso* took a few *soles* out of his coca pouch, counted them out one by one until there were ten, and asked someone to go out and see where he could get some liquor.

"I want everything done right for poor Damián."

The shadows were deepening and around the corpse burned four candles—a gift from Doña Melcha—protected from the wind by an improvised curtain of ponchos. Near the door, dimly lighting the group of mourners on the porch, stood two pans in which wicks were burning in suet.

As the wind whipped the flickering lights about, the shadows came leaping toward the cabin and then, when it calmed down and the lights burned steadily again, they crowded back again beyond the hut.

In the distance the howls of dogs could be heard.

After an abundant supper, by the pale light of the wicks, they went on drinking and chewing coca. Rum, which on other occasions became talk or crying or laughter or song, now, in the presence of a corpse, became silence. The tight silence of mouths that have only a small register of grief. They had done their simple mourning, and now all there was left for them to do was to be silent until the hour of prayer.

Over to one side the river roared suddenly. Near by a katydid kept up its unvarying song, and the rain dripped on the leaves of the trees. The near-by trickles of water gleamed like streaks of silver and farther off, night spread over the valley, black and tragic as a shroud.

New howls were heard. A puppy that had followed one of the *cholos* got up and went running toward the corpse, sniffed at it, then barked at the shadows and finally let out a long, piteous howl. A whiplash of fear seemed to cut through all the mourners, and Doña Melcha, who had been in one of the inside rooms of the house, rushed out, shouting anxiously: "Let us pray, Christians, let us pray for this soul which must be in torment."

The women knelt down around the dead man, and the men formed another close kneeling circle around them. The lights projected enlarged shadows of poncho-covered backs and hairy heads against the walls. And the usual prayer rose to the lips of all, lips trembling with sorrow: "Our Father . . . thy kingdom come . . . on earth as it is in Heaven . . . give us this day . . . and forgive us our trespasses . . . amen."

It was a lugubrious, monotonous music, sadder even than the howling of the dogs, sorrow, and death; but that incantation of faith comforted the soul. When the prayer was finished, the *cholos* sat down quietly, serene once more, and again the jugs of rum passed from hand to hand and from mouth to mouth.

In one of the inner rooms Doña Melcha and the other women went on praying, but this time it was for "travelers and sailors, the sick and the poor." Then a sharp scream came piercing the night: "Umaaa . . . umaaa."

All the dogs in the valley started to bark.

"Umaaa . . . umaaa," the scream quivered on.

The mourners exchanged opinions. It must have been the puma which, according to Doña Mariana, prowled around her flock sometimes at night. Arturo went for his revolver, and when he came back he and Encarna ran down the valley, until they were lost in the darkness.

"Umaaa . . . umaaa."

The dogs kept up their ear-splitting noise in every key. We had forgotten about the dead man and his soul and thought only about the menace of this wild beast. This whipped up the blood until it boiled. What was death in the face of life, the beloved life of the animals that belonged to man, whom he should protect and care for at all costs? Now he was taking the goats; afterward it would be the asses and the horses. The comments grew more enraged, and the other *cholos,* after swearing by Christ and the souls of the Blessed, rushed off toward Doña Mariana's house, too, armed with sticks and determination. The night was pitch black, and the animal might have run off already, but that made no difference to the belligerent, aroused fighters.

At intervals echoes of voices and shouts floated back to us and we waited the return of the hunters in taut anxiety. When the pink, milky morning showed itself above the treetops, from which belated drops of water were still falling, the *cholos* returned with scowling, disappointed faces.

"It was that damned puma and, to make things worse, it took a goat."

"We'll have to lay for it another night."

Arturo passed terse judgment, looking at his rusty revolver: "All five bullets right in the back of the neck."

When the day was well up we carried the dead man on our shoulders to the cemetery, and began to dig his grave. The women were still praying around the corpse which had been laid under the fragrant foliage of an orange tree.

The damp earth gave off a fresh smell as we deepened the hole, and when the dirt, in which a few old mouldering bones could be seen, no longer gleamed as it was spaded up, the diggers got out and the corpse was lowered by ropes into the grave.

The *utoso* bade his companion farewell with a few handfulls of earth which he slowly scattered the full length of the grave, and then the shovels finished up the burial. In a little while a gray rectangle lay in the midst of the lush grass of the cemetery. Finally a bare wooden cross was put at the head. In time it would disappear amid the grass and would finally fall, its ropes rotted and its wood decayed.

On our way back we finished up the rum we had left, and when we got home the *utoso* gathered up the dead man's poncho and saddlebags, and his own. Then he took his leave:

"Well, good-bye. May God repay you, gentlemen."

Arturo asked him: "Aren't you going to Huama-chuco?"

The man looked at him without answering a word, while Arturo went on urging him.

"You go to Huamachuco, and get cured there."

"If you haven't any money, we'll take you across without charging you for it. Come on, you ought to go."

With a great effort, after thinking the matter over for a moment, the sick man tried to explain what he felt.

"What for? I'm about ready to die. What do I want to go for now? My friend wasn't able to cross the river and I have a feeling that I won't either. And to go so far from home. . . . What hope that I'd ever get there!"

And taking the road to the hills, he expressed his gratitude once more: "May God repay you, gentlemen. . . . May God repay you."

Toward Condormarca, to die there in his own country and not to have to pass the river of these endless valleys which to him were *uta* and death. The flies swarmed after him buzzing about his foul flesh. He walked ahead slowly without looking around, supporting himself on his stout cane.

The puma returned the next night. And the next. And the next. The *cholos* talked of nothing but the damage it had done, cursing the useless clubs and machetes, the guns that jammed and the revolvers that missed.

"That animal has a charmed life."

"We'll get it yet."

It went into Doña Mariana's fold time after time. Encarna had spent the night with his gun at the foot of a cedar tree, and when the animal showed up and he was ready to shoot, the gun did not go off and the only sound was the idle click of the hammer. Arturo who was lying in wait, along the side of the fence, shot twice but only managed to kill two goats.

The goats had to be eaten up, and they took them to Doña Mariana's cabin. She cooked them to perfection to see if the hunters would show their appreciation and really catch the marauder.

"He won't get away tonight," Arturo assured her.

"Fellows," said Encarna to the circle of hungry *cholos* that had gathered around the great platter of stew and yuccas like a band of condors around their prey, "fellows," (here he choked on a big bite he had taken), "I want to tell you that the puma I saw had a sort of a bluish look, about the color of indigo. Maybe it's an enchanted puma."

Simon Chancahuana, who had been armed with a club which proved useless, as the puma passed on the

opposite side—as was to be expected with the eyesight
and shrewdness they've got—laughed loudly:

"Charmed, charmed, my foot. It's the dark that
makes him look like that. I don't believe there's any
difference between this puma and any other one around
here."

But Arturo could not understand how he came to
miss.

"I have always hit the mark with my old revolver,
and I can't help thinking it's queer that I missed."

Then he told boastingly how, one time, he brought
down an eagle on the wing with a shot through the
breast, and that another time he shot a heron's head off
and that any time at fifteen paces he could bring down
an alligator pear shooting it through the stem. And finally he said:

"If this is a puma like any other, this is going to be
its last night."

And night came. The valley slept under the shadows
and the rain, but in Doña Mariana's fields an anxious
vigil was being kept. When Hormecinda heard Matarrayo bark, she whimpered like a young goat, grieving
for the flocks which she followed day after day, carrying the newborn kids on her back, lavishing the greatest
care upon them, taking them back and forth over these
hills covered with underbrush and shrubs. And now a
wicked puma had come to destroy them. Doña Mariana
listened in silence, calling upon all the saints in the
calendar not to let it be an enchanted puma. In the
fold the goats ran from one side to the other at the least
sound, and in a corner, Arturo lay hidden under the
skins of the goats that he himself had killed, with his
revolver in hand.

In that uncomfortable position, soaked through by the
rain, it seemed to him that the hours dragged on endlessly. The night was pitch black and only a pale diffuse
blotch of gray indicated the presence of goats. The wind
was whistling. Was that someone faintly crying? Arturo
began to feel a certain uneasiness, a strange fear. No
question about it, he could hear a sharp groan, which

came and went, disappeared and then began anew. Could it be the sobbing of a soul in torment? There was no doubt about it. What about the puma? Queer how he missed his aim. Could there be witchcraft mixed up in the affair? And if that were the case, wouldn't it bring him bad luck? There had been cases where men wasted away to a shadow, and nobody knew why, and that in spite of the fact that they ate a lot because they were as hungry as a buzzard all the time. And then they died. . . . And these men were always talking about enchanted lakes and mountains and rivers and pumas. And everything had happened to them at sunset or during the night. What if something like that were to happen to him? . . .

Suddenly, in the midst of these dismal thoughts he was surprised by a swift blur that jumped over the fence as the goats crowded together on the other side, bleating desperately. Arturo was so unnerved by the sudden apparition, by the fires and the night, that he thought the puma itself looked blue. It seemed to give off a blue radiance. He kept on firing the revolver but, in which direction? The night was alive with shot and barks which the crags re-echoed, while the puma made off with a bleating kid between its jaws.

When Doña Mariana appeared at the door Arturo was already there, panting, hoarse, and his voice sounding as though his diaphragm were tense with horror.

"Blue . . . it's blue . . . an enchanted puma."

There was no sleep for Calemar. The enchanted puma roamed the valley in all directions, his blue shadow slinking past the houses in the darkness. And every day his depredations grew worse.

He attacked the fold that belonged to the Carpenas and killed four goats just for the fun of it. Out in a pasture one morning they found a donkey with its throat slashed open by the puma's fierce claws and its breast eaten away. One dog that was bolder than the others died, too, from a bite that ripped out its windpipe. The blue puma spread death and terror on every side.

The horses and the donkeys now spent the night beside the house door, and although the dogs were beaten to make them stay with the flocks, the minute they heard the beast they came rushing out, barking in fear, and rubbing up against their master's legs.

Rifle reports blazed out like flashes of lightning but all they did was gleam. Arturo's revolver had passed from hand to hand, uselessly, just to try it out. Those who had seen the eyes of the puma glitter in the darkness were few, as usually happens, but they were all certain that it was blue, bluer than the sky. It was the dark blue of the river, but with a bright, burning magic gleam.

It was not only the neighing, the bleating, the shouting and shooting that gave evidence of the presence of the beast. Even the patter of the rain, the trembling of the leaves, the whistle of the wind and the bellow of the river spoke of the blue puma.

The men watched, arms in hand, in the now feeble shelter of the cabins, beside the women who prayed to the Virgin of Perpetual Help, to St. Anthony, and especially to St. Rita of Cassia, who could bring to pass the impossible, to intercede with God to destroy or drive away the beast.

But the woods turned blue at the passing of the enchanted puma, which roved the countryside, invulnerable and devastating, destroying life at will. He now attacked just for the pleasure of killing and sucking the blood, for he was glutted with food.

Arturo was not feeling well. He said that ever since he saw the puma for the second time and came under the spell of its glow he had felt weak and he dreamed over and over that a great blue blur crept up to him, spread over him and smothered him.

God only knows what Doña Mariana, way down at the foot of the valley, was doing. Nobody went down there to help her out, for right after Arturo's failure, when a group of *cholos,* headed by Lieutenant Governor Florencio, surrounded one fold the puma calmly raided the other. No doubt this was because it did not want to lay a spell on all of them. The animal had increased its range of activities and now, as far as he could, everybody looked after his own.

But Doña Mariana had done a lot. She had not been sitting with her hands folded in her lap, or just joined in prayer. She had lain in wait night after night until she discovered the place at the foot of the stockade where the animal got through by giving a high agile leap. Then she thought of two *chonta* sticks that Abdón from Celendín had left behind him, and she spent three days sharpening them on a stone, for the wood is hard as rock and the first blows had dented her machete.

The *chonta* sticks had been stuck in the place where the beast should come down after his jump.

The night was black with rain and the river hurled itself along cursing. The men, in the darkness of their cabins, rattled their clubs and machetes from time to time. The dogs barked but the flocks were quiet. There was none of that distressed bleating which denoted the presence of the beast. The horses and donkeys were loosely tied to the posts and pillars around the house, and they munched contentedly at the fodder piled up before them.

Doña Mariana, squatting behind the door of her cabin, with Hormecinda crouching beside her, for she had not been able to close her eyes since the terrible animal began destroying her beloved flock, kept watch. Matarrayo was with them but he was unable to give the least bark because of the tight muzzle he was wearing.

The hours slipped by slowly, silently, because the drip of rain and the roaring of the river were so monotonous that they were like silence. "You can't hear a sound, "Doña Mariana whispered in Hormecinda's ear. Could the devilish beast have scented danger?

The vigil dragged on, and it must have been very late, because some cocks were beginning to crow when the goats began to bleat and mill around, bumping their heads against the stockade. The dogs were barking angrily and fearfully when suddenly a frenzied roar was heard. The goats in the barn lot bleated with terror while Matarrayo trembled as he struggled to get his jaws open.

There it is! There it is! The beast kept on roaring. Now it was caught.

Doña Mariana felt as though a great weight had fallen from her shoulders, and Hormecinda sobbed with piercing, choking cries, almost hysterical with relief. In the fold the bleating of the goats continued, and the roars died down for a moment, suddenly became furious howls, and then died down again.

It was caught. But maybe it wasn't. Maybe the beast was just roaring because it had been wounded and now in its rage it was tearing the herd to pieces. The night which confounded and smothered everything in its shadows was a thick, black brutal night, a night made for witchcraft and enchantment. No, it was no good going to the fold, and it would be better to wait till morning and let the light reveal the good or the bad news.

The dogs in the other houses kept on barking, and the women, as they listened to them, redoubled the fervor of their prayers and the men pounded their clubs on the ground and clashed their machetes together still louder as they shouted: "Umaaa . . . umaaa."

The whole night was one long-drawn-out howl.

The morning was just breaking into a pale color when Doña Mariana stepped cautiously out and peered through the cracks of the stockade. There was the puma where it had fallen on the *chonta* sticks. God in heaven!

The beast had been run through the belly by one of the sticks and was roaring and writhing to no avail, trying to get loose, when it became aware of the woman's presence. The ground was a pool of blood. Doña Mariana's rage turned her eyes into living coals, she grabbed up a club, and rushed into the field, while Hormecinda screamed at the top of her lungs: "It's caught . . . caught . . . come over."

The *cholos,* with their wives following at their heels, rushed out of their cabins and when they got to Doña Mariana's pen, she was still beating the puma over the head, which was nothing but a bloody mass. She picked up a big stone and with her trembling hands let it drop and the brains splattered in all directions. But in case that was not enough, Doña Mariana picked up a club once more and beat it over the muzzle, the back, the paws, the belly.

"Take this, you devil; take this, you marauder, and this, and this."

When she finally realized that the puma would never get up again, and that everybody was standing around looking at her, she straightened up, brandishing the club and shouting peals of laughter.

"A blue puma . . . a blue puma they called it."

She went on laughing and swinging the club as though she were about to lay somebody's head open, and added: "It's like all the others . . . half brown and half yellow . . . the blue puma!"

The valley people could not get over their amazement. If it weren't for the fact that they had to keep one eye on Doña Mariana, who was in a mood to club somebody just for the fun of it, their astonishment would have been still greater. Nevertheless they stood with eyes like saucers gazing upon the mass of wounded flesh which had kept them up so many nights. Arturo, when he saw that there was no blue puma, laughed at his enchantment and got well instantly.

"Ha-ha . . . ha-ha-ha," Doña Mariana went on laughing, the same Doña Mariana once so melancholy. Then she jumped up and down. Anybody would have said she had lost her mind.

13

The Landslide

The grass was invading the planted patches and as soon as the rain let up a little we would have to go into our gardens, grub hoe in hand, and begin a long, stubborn struggle.

The light gleamed upon the steel of the implements, the faces of the *cholos,* bright with sweat, the plumage of the birds which left their hiding places and came out to sing again, and the leaves of the trees, turgid and clean.

Finally the green of the coca bushes, the yucca and the chile stood out luxuriantly above the black beds of cultivated earth. But right behind the hoers, row upon row, the grass sprouted again with undiminished vigor from the ground soaked with water and sheltered by the thick canebrake. And the sun was hot, even though fleeting.

And while the back was bowed and the hoe turned up the earth, from clod, patch of grass, limb of bush, some snake was coiling to strike. You had to be on watch against their attack continually, and then find a long stick to finish them off. Yellow, brown, green snakes crawled and coiled themselves in the planted plots. They swung themselves from limb to limb, from tree to tree, and God help the person who got bitten: he could tell the world good-bye.

But the letup of the rain lasted only a short time and soon the people had to shut themselves up in their cabins again. And there was nothing to do but watch it come down. The recollection of the blue puma lasted for a long time, enlivening the coca-chewing mouths of the *cholos*. With the rain falling in torrents outside, it was a dramatic theme for the long nights until finally it wore itself out.

Of late, we had had little to think of except ferrying and weeding, but that was no longer the case since Don Matías had returned from the trip he made to Bambamarca for salt. He brought back the news of a possible landslide. No sooner had he lifted the little sack of salt from his donkey than the seasoned old fellow who never missed a trick and could smell danger a mile off said: "I don't like the look of those slopes of the ravine. You can call me a liar if we don't have a landslide here any day now when we get a hard rain."

And then he added, while all who listened watched him intently: "All those slopes are loose, half cracked, no more body to them than foam."

A landslide is a dangerous thing. What happens is that the rain loosens the dirt on the slopes of the hills and suddenly, in certain places, it cannot hold any longer and slides down into the gulches and valleys. The noise it makes, when a storm is going on, resembles the echo of distant thunderclaps, and only the dogs can tell the difference. Over by Cionera, some years ago, a shepherd and his flock were buried under a thick layer of stones and mud at the bottom of a gap. But on the crags which surround Calemar there had never been a landslide, and the only danger was that it might occur farther up, on the sides sloping down to the ravine. Then the stream at the bottom, swollen by the storm, would drag the avalanche along toward the valley.

After warning of the danger, Don Matías mourned: "What a shame my Chusquito died from getting into the habit of eating crickets. Otherwise that fellow would be barking the minute he heard a landslide."

But there were other dogs who gave warning. Those native dogs with their bleary eyes and tangled hair lived close beside their masters—eyes and ears alert—to warn them of danger, and barking and restless the moment anything out of the ordinary happened.

Now, after the old man's warning, with the claps of thunder so deadened by the storm and the distance that they could be differentiated only by the dogs, the rainy season became a time that weighed on our hearts like the hand of death.

It was different with the river. With our paddles in hand on the rafts which knew our strength, on the water which—because it was as old as the river—also knew our courage, we laughed at death.

But there is no defense against landslides. Who can stop a falling hill with a few logs and a paddle, however skillfully they are managed by stout-hearted valley men who never give up?

And withal, we would have to fight.

The morning was like any other after the stormy night, and old Matías was talking with his wife: the price of salt had gone up because they said that the rain melted it when it was brought in and also the dampness in the warehouses during the rainy season; it looked as though there would be a good crop of yuccas, the *sinamomos* were getting scarce because people were cutting them down without any consideration.

The rain had not yet cleared up, but was falling less heavily, letting down a thin curtain and pouring off the trees with every gust of wind. The brook in the bottom of the ravine hurled its swollen waters over the rocks where it emptied into the Marañón, which was already so swollen that it paid no attention to this increase. The river beds were full and the trees and reeds along the banks were falling as their roots lost their grip on the earth that grew damper and looser by the minute.

"What about that fellow, Don Osvaldo," recalled old

Melcha, listening to the roaring of the brook, a clear sign that it was raining violently up in the highlands.

We had often thought about Don Osvaldo. Nobody had heard anything about him since he left, but now the old man was able to supply us with certain information.

"He's up there staying with somebody. They told me in Bambamarca that he was looking for mines and that his sorrel had slipped and broken a leg."

Doña Melcha served the old man a second helping of hot soup for his breakfast and then he prepared for the day's work. This consisted of sitting at the door of his cabin, chewing away at his coca, plaiting a rope or talking with any visitor who happened by. Suddenly a violent deafening noise—this one was close—came to his ears, like the reverberation of a damp drum.

It was a loud clap which brought the old man to his feet and turned his eyes instinctively toward the cliffs. These stood there, the steadiness of their rocks unshaken, and the old man realized that what he predicted had come to pass, and he came running first to my hut and then to the others, shouting: "A landslide in the ravine. Machetes and axes."

The word passed from one person to the next and the valley came alive with cries. "Machetes."

"Machetes."

"Axes."

"A landslide."

"Hurry to the ravine."

"Come on."

The men went running to the ravine, their tools in hand, through the rain, up the muddy paths, the branches of the trees gushing water on them as they touched them. A group gathered on either bank, quickly, while the old man shouted directions for the work they were to do.

"Cut down trees!"

They began at the spot where the brook descended to the valley, spilling over the rocks. Axes and machetes kept up a quick crackling, splitting the base of the tree trunks. White chips flew through the air, and the trees creaked and toppled over. *Sinamomos,* alligator pears, *gualangos, arabiscos,* even cedars, piled up their branches and trunks at a certain distance from both banks.

The water of the brook diminished for a moment, probably because it was held back momentarily by the landslide, when suddenly it seemed as though the whole mountainside were coming toward us through the brook's channel. The water rushed ahead in oily waves, mounting higher each time, and increasingly dangerous because it carried clay, boulders and rubble which kept filling up the bed.

The great convulsive yellowish mass swelled quickly and made it seem as though all the trees in the valley would not be enough to check it. Up at the top, where it started, it ran off to the side, for it had filled up the bed of the stream and the layer of stones and clay spread out beyond the breakwater we had tried to form with the trees. The flood spread farther still; the swollen waters ran through the valley, tugging at the big trees, and breaking and uprooting bushes and bamboos.

As it came down the middle the landslide filled up the bed there, too, and overflowed, flooding the planted fields. Silverio Cruz, his wife and his young son, rushed toward their cabin and hurriedly dragged out bundles of blankets, pots and implements, putting them on top of a low hill. And not a moment too soon, for the mountain of waters swept over the house, tearing down the reed walls and the beams and corner posts that had held up the roof, which floated for a moment before it was sucked under by the mud. Every minute the waters spread out wider and wider, the fences broke down and the crops disappeared from the fields, where huge trees were left behind as though they had grown there. It was the plum season, and thousands of the red fruit went bobbing along in the muddy water in which a number of snakes could be seen writhing.

On one side and down the valley, because the other side is higher, the landslide rushed until it met the

Marañón, completely engulfing Silverio's farm and covering it with stones.

Not a word did the *cholo* say. He looked at his wife and at his little boy, and then at us, as if to ask why it should have been his misfortune to have his garden and his hut disappear this way, but his lips were mute.

The landslide finally came to an end, as the hours went by, the brook dug its channel again and reunited its waters. By evening it was a strip running through the center of the avalanche, and tomorrow or the next day it would have its deep bed again. The rain washed away the mud and, after a few hours, we could see that Silverio's field was nothing but a bluish mass of stones and rubble. There was no possibility of planting there again, because it would have been impossible to clear away all those stones.

Silverio, his wife and little boy took refuge in Jacinto Huamán's house. The rain kept on steadily. In the distance we heard the hoarse growl of the river. From the fields arose the smell of mud from the landslide.

In talking over what he was to do, Silverio said: "Now I'll just be a ferryman."

His wife inquired about a house.

"I'll build it on a piece of land that doesn't belong to anybody, on the upper side of the flume."

The wild roaring of the river was to Silverio's ears a song of calm and assurance, and he repeated, serenely and firmly: "I'll be a ferryman—what more do I want?"

14

The Lonely Raft

"River Marañón, let me cross." The strong, uninterrupted splashing of the oars brought the song to our minds. "River Marañon, I have to cross." The rolled-up sleeves showed the dark, sinewy forearms. The muscles, on which heavy veins stood out, rose and fell. Crossing or returning, the paddles dipped noisily into the water, moving the raft ahead. It rose and fell on the dark waves, avoiding treacherous logs which hid below the water, leaving only an occasional branch in view, shooting rapids, evading hidden rocks, creaking, jolting . . . always forward.

"River Marañón, let me cross." The flexible torsos curved a little over the water. The bronzed faces were set in an expression of determination, and over them fell locks of straight, black hair, gleaming in the sun or jet-black in the rain. "River Marañón, I have to cross."

Their knees flexed as in prayer, steadying themselves against the joining of the logs heavy with water from their continual usage, they and the passengers who huddled together in the middle, fearfully watching the swollen, convulsive, greedy river, all seemed to say, as with one voice, "River Marañón, let me cross."

This scene was constantly repeated.

It so happened that one afternoon we had ferried

across a civil guard who was going to Cajamarquilla, a merchant from Celendín and two Indians.

When we got to our side we were dripping wet because it had started to rain as we began to cross. The travelers were anxious to get to their lodging for the night as quickly as they could, and they went off as soon as we reached land, but we had to pull the raft ashore. We pulled it up the smooth runway of logs, and soon had it out of reach of the river. Just to be on the safe side we tied it to an alligator pear tree.

We were just ready to leave, too, when we saw a raft drift by, more than halfway to the other side. It was not coming across but was heading down stream, and there was nobody on it.

It was a stray raft that had come who knows whence and would wind up God knows where. Perhaps the water would carry it still closer to the bank and wash it against the big rocks that jutted out or into the rocky inlets and pull it apart and tear it to pieces. It might be that some ferryman would be crossing the river just then and could get hold of it, or that a good swimmer would see it coming in time to swim out and get it. But now it was even with us and to swim out toward it would just be a waste of time.

And not one thing to be seen on the rocking framework. We screwed up our eyes the better to see, but it was always the same—not a poncho, nor a saddlebag, nor any sign of the owner. It seemed as though it had come from far away and that it must have gotten very wet, for the brown of the logs had taken on a dark tone.

What had happened to it? Could it have been jerked loose from its mooring place by a sudden swift current? Or caught in a jam and the men navigating it had to jump into the water, struggling through the mass of logs and brush? If so, they died or were saved depending on their agility and their fate. Maybe they were riding it down the river and it crashed against a cliff or got caught in an eddy or whirlpool and for that reason it was alone.

The raft skimmed along over the waters on its course.

Now it disappeared from sight, dwarfed by the distance and the majestic breadth of the river. Finally it was lost in the twilight and the darkness of the waters, leaving only a blur.

When we reached our houses we told what we had seen, and our food was as ashes on our tongues, and our every act was a requiem to express that for which words failed us.

Only the men of these valleys, the people along the Marañón, know and understand the tragic message spelled by a few logs bound together drifting downstream, by a lost, lone raft.

15

The Return of Don Osvaldo

As though to prove to us that he was still alive, Don Osvaldo Martínez de Calderón returned to the valley one afternoon, riding a shaggy dappled-gray pony, which he tried in vain to spur on to a smart trot. It plodded along with its head to the ground, and the rider's where its own should have been. Slowly, at a calm, sober amble it rounded the curves of the sloping descent, came down the middle of the street and stopped in front of the house of Don Matías.

The young man from Lima wore a simple bandanna around his neck. His clothes were in tatters and his boots were badly worn where the straps of the stirrups rubbed them. Only his revolver gleamed as on the first visit, although the holster was creased and dull. His hands and face were burned from the cold and the sharp lash of the wind.

"Come in, Don Osvaldo, come in."

He dismounted slowly while Arturo took charge of the horse and unfastened its bridle. When he loosened the cinch the horse heaved a long sigh and gave its whole shabby body a good shake. Its haunch was roughly scarred by the wide burn of the branding iron.

"This gray must be Don Juan's," remarked Arturo at the sight of the huge J P branded on the beast.

"That's right," answered Don Osvaldo, sitting on

the edge of the porch, "he loaned it to me. He is a fine man who helped me in every way he could. If it hadn't been for him, it would have been the end of the trail for me."

"What about the sorrel? They say he slipped and fell."

"Oh, it's a long story. Yes, he did slip over one of those devilish precipice roads. . . ."

"Then I'll bet you've got plenty of news to tell," remarked old Matías, winking a sly eye.

"You bet I have. This is a fine place to collect news. How has everything been around here?"

"We've got plenty, too. One is that Roge never came back from Shicún."

The engineer frowned inquiringly.

"Yes, the water swallowed him up when the poor lad . . ."

The sun had sunk behind the peaks across the river, and darkness came creeping up the canebrake, crawling through the bushes. The birds chirped as they sought their nests, and everything was enveloped in that heavy lethargy that comes over the valleys of the Marañón at nightfall. A herd of goats passed through the street and two young bucks stopped there for a long time in a stubborn monotonous fight, neither one wanting to give in. Hormecinda whistled stones past the ears of those of the herd that tried to get into the gardens and the rest trotted along, bleating and jumping up to try and nibble the branches of the trees, until they disappeared from sight along the path that led to their fold.

Don Osvaldo had kept his eyes intently fixed on the girl. And there was reason for it. Her fifteen years frolicked through her slender yet solid body. Her wide wool skirt could no longer conceal the rounded curve of her hips, and inside her coarse cotton blouse her imprisoned breasts seemed to flutter, breathless with anxiety. Her merry face was a clear pale brown, and her eyes were like a dark night full of fireflies.

"Who is that girl?"

"That's Hormecinda, the niece of Doña Mariana. . . ."

"I don't know any more than I did when we started. Where does she graze her goats?" the engineer went on.

Old Matías smiled a waggish smile and answered: "Why, over there in that field, where else could it be?"

But Don Osvaldo answered very seriously: "But I don't see much pasture around here, and I don't see them in the meadows with the horses and donkeys."

Arturo realized that the engineer was pretending to be stupid and he said: "What? Didn't you know that they eat nothing but stones?"

Because of Lucinda, who was about to make an addition to the family, Arturo went home early to his cabin where Doña Melcha was burning Heaven knows what herbs, whose subtle aroma reached all the way to us. The old man had cooked dinner and also served it, setting out everything just so, for "a Christian who's been around has to know a little of everything."

"Well, Don Osvaldo, and what you been doing up there all this time? It's been a year since you first came."

The engineer ate his food with relish, and when he had swallowed a big mouthful, he answered: "I couldn't say myself. At first I thought I'd be there a month or two. Afterwards I stayed on one day, and another until, you see for yourself, how long I've been there. I can't understand it myself."

"So that's it, and here we were saying, what's happened to him that he does not come back. Who knows but what he may be dead?"

"You're right. Life is very hard up there. And how about your people?"

"Pretty much the same. I told you about what happened to my boy Roge in the summer. Then things went along without much change, but this winter— Jesus Christ. When I tell you that we even saw a blue puma. . . . The *cholo* Encarna began the story and then Arturo also said that he had seen it. And then everybody saw it, the blue puma, the blue puma . . ."

The old man related the story in all its details and then we laughed heartily when the engineer added:

"Naturally, the blaze of the shots he fired made everything look blue to Arturo . . ."

The talk rambled here and there. The old man recalled everything important that had happened, and comments and suppositions came thick and fast. The nights along the Marañón, with their overpowering, motionless heat, were fine for conversation till sleep came. Besides, we enjoyed going over our troubles, recalling our difficulties, and adding new touches to our commonplace, daily existence.

After we had eaten it was out of the question to think of staying in the cabin. A cloud of mosquitoes swarmed about burying their fiery stings into us. Smoke was not enough to halt the assault, and there was danger that Don Osvaldo might get malaria. He had no mosquito net this time, for it had gone into the abyss with the sorrel, and he kept ceaselessly slapping at the insects trying to kill them. He could not have slept anyway for their persistent buzzing made it impossible even for the natives to sleep. If you were under the net it was not too bad to have to listen to their whining buzz; but without it, they could exasperate you half out of your wits.

"We'd better go down by the river," the old man advised.

"The river?" exclaimed Don Osvaldo.

"Yes," he answered, "there the wind blows them away."

Each of us took a poncho and a blanket. As we walked along, pursued by the relentless buzzing, the old man went on explaining to the engineer.

"This is the season for the mosquitoes. In the stagnant pools left after the rainy season they breed so fast you can't imagine what it's like. After a few days these buzzing around now will be dead, the swamps will dry up, and then there'll just be the usual number, so folks won't say we don't have any here."

In a little while we settled ourselves on the sand of the bank. The heat came through our blankets for the sun had been blazing down on it all day. The waning

moon shone overhead through thin fleecy clouds and
the river murmured softly, soothing us to sleep with
its cradlesong. A cool refreshing breeze blew past,
whispering in a low voice to the trees.

We chewed our coca and the engineer, after listening a moment to the rattling of our lime gourds said:
"Pass me some of that coca, too!"

"So you've learned already."

"Let me tell you if it hadn't been for it I would have
died up on Campana Ridge."

We pulled out our pouches and he took a little from
each. After rolling it around his mouth to moisten it,
he slipped the wad into his cheek. Then he took our
lime gourds, too, and the very wires we used and he
talked the way we do, taking a chew at his wad between words.

"I'm going to tell you something, Don Oshva," said
old Matías with great satisfaction, "a person who
learns to chew coca in these parts stays here. The coca
makes him belong to these valleys and these highlands."

The old man pointed to the cliffs that reached upward. The pale moon turned them into huge blocks of
darkness. At their foot, in front of us, ran the river,
a swath of silver, beside which the rocks at times took
on human semblance.

"*Quién sabe?* I had a bad time of it at first, but
now I'm getting used to it."

We didn't say anything, but it gratified us to see this
city gentleman chewing coca like any one of us valley
fellows, for he seemed closer to us, a man fit to cope
with the ferocity of our land. In a little while he began
twisting around in his place in a nervous way that was
not usual in him. It was the effect of the coca on one
who was not accustomed to it. He kept on talking and
he watched the river with eyes filled with growing astonishment. He was seeing the valley all over again under
the spell of the potent leaf.

"The river, yes, the river," he exclaimed.

Under the veiled light of the moon, the river went

rippling past. Its white foam made a lace edge all along the bank. The engineer turned his eyes to the valley, to the thick, murmuring groves. The rustle of the leaves was accompanied by the call of the hoot owls. Far away a screech owl began to cry and others answered, filling the night with their mournful wail.

"The river, yes, the river," said the engineer looking back at it once more. "I never thought of it. It is so large, so masterful and it has made all this, hasn't it? It has hollowed out these valleys with the fury of its rage, which has terrified even the overwhelming mass of the hills. It has sawed out the peaks and cut open the ravines. The centuries it has spent frolicking about here and there until it has dug its channel and left the valley to one side. Then it bursts forth where it will and washes away the valleys themselves. If it were not for that great cliff up there, do you think you would be here? Indeed you would not! But I should not be surprised if one day it tore that away, or a gigantic flood should overflow it and Calemar would become nothing but a pebble-covered strand. With the passing of time, *gualangos* will spring up, and it will be like any other beach, without a sign of cultivated fields, without a sign of man. . . ."

We, too, thought this could happen and that the river could do all this and a great deal more. But the conflict between water and rock would not be settled so soon and that cliff which reached up to the beginning of the sierra was strong, too, and the struggle could last an eternity.

The engineer went on, noisily chewing his coca: "All this is terrific. I have gone through a lot and I have searched all over. It's companies, big companies that are needed to overcome this wilderness. Everything is here and nothing is here. I have explored it well. The basin of the Huayabamba, famous for its natural wealth, needs a railroad or a highway which would have to go up and around all those damned rocks and would cost a mint of money. Can you imagine? There are mines up there in those heights but what about the machinery? The things I have been through looking for those mines, what I have seen, what I have heard!"

"Tell us, Don Oshva, come on, tell us what you saw," coaxed the old man.

"Nothing and everything. Well, it was hack and hack away at those jagged mountain ridges, eating badly, sleeping badly. One day my horse slipped over the mountainside, I was left without my mosquito net, and the frost was searing me. Another day there wasn't a cloud in the sky and the Indian with me said: 'It's going to rain, *taita*.' I just laughed at him and told him to get started when, right out there in the midst of the mountains the sky suddenly turned black, a terrible storm burst over us, and we could not move, and got soaked to the skin. I can't understand how I'm still alive. Another day I was in Bambamarca and I wanted to go out at night. 'No, señorcito,' the Indian Aristobulo who was governor answered, 'tonight is the night the woman who was burned at the stake walks the streets of the village in torment.' I asked him how a reservist like him—for Aristobulo has done his military service and has a little education, and, above all, a desire to get on in the world—who had been on the coast and all over, could believe in such nonsense. All I could get out of him was: 'That's the way it is, sir, that's the way it is.' And you know what it was all about? The burned woman was a woman who had been sentenced to death by fire."

"Yes, yes, we know," we all answered.

But memories were still worrying the enginer. The owls hooted mournfully and he felt a sense of uneasiness all through him. His hands kept moving around as though they were looking for something to catch hold of. Finally he began to talk again.

"Well, in a town there was a priest by the name of Ruiz. This priest had a woman and a son who was almost grown. Another Indian woman in the town, very good-looking and said to be a witch, got tangled up with the priest, too. Did you ever hear of such a thing? A priest doing such things!"

"Out here a priest always has himself a woman."

"I know, I know, out here they do all such things, and as bold as brass about it, too. Well, that was the way things were, when one day the good-looking girl butchered a pig and the priest's son went to ask her for cracklings. 'Give me just one,' he begged, in that tone they use which gets on my nerves. 'There aren't any, there aren't any,' she answered, but the boy kept on and finally she gave him some. He ate them and then he went out and drank a lot of water and stuffed himself on green fruit. Then he got an attack of colic and died in a little while. The mother began to nag at the priest one day and the next day, till finally she convinced him. So the priest, one Sunday after Mass, told the people they ought to burn the witch whom he had already put in the custody of the governor. The whole town went out to the fields and brought wood into the middle of the square to build a huge pyre. The woman was brought out. She was beside herself crying and swearing that she had not done anything wrong. They tied her hand and foot and put her on that huge pile of wood. They lighted it at each corner, and in a minute the devouring flames were licking at the poor creature who was writhing like a snake begging them for the love of God to take her out of there. But the Indians, instead of taking her out, were standing around with clubs to finish her off if she should manage to get loose. The flames and the smoke were burning her to a crisp and smothering her. Her moans died away, but the Indians kept throwing on wood, for the wife of the priest, pale and disheveled, kept egging them on to a savage fury, shouting that they must get rid of that devil's paramour. The priest, standing behind the pyre, was praying in a low voice and his trembling hands could hardly tell the beads of his rosary. . . ."

The engineer helped himself to more coca and went on: "An hour later there was nothing left but ashes.

Ever since then there has been a barren spot in the square. Not even the tiniest plant or blade of grass has grown again on that scorched clay. I've seen it with my own eyes."

"We've seen it, too."

"Everything I've told you was told to me by Aristobulo, while the night outside grew blacker and great blasts of wind howled by. Will you believe that I didn't go out that night? I walked two steps from the door and then turned back. I was afraid. At midnight I woke up with a start and it seemed to me I could hear cries and laments all through the town. What could it be? The howling of the wind, perhaps? But, on my word of honor, it was just like the weeping of a woman."

The wind had cooled our foreheads and the heat of the sand had died away. It would be good to sleep now, but uneasiness had dug its claws into our souls, and we would have to talk on a while till sleep could find rest.

The old man said: "Don Oshva, who understands this matter of torment? The soul suffers when it departs in such a way, and comes back for us Christians to comfort it, but the trouble is that it frightens us. When we talk about them, they come back, too. The witch must be around somewhere. Don't you notice how you're afraid?"

And, it was true, we felt a vague fear. Something was hovering about us, like a mysterious vapor, present yet not present. But it was there, looking at us, perhaps, beseeching us. The burned woman, without doubt. The hooting of the owls became terrifying.

Don Matías advised: "You must make the sign of the Blessed Cross in the air. . . ."

And he traced the sign of the cross in the air with his gnarled forefinger. In silence the engineer stretched out his slender hand and did the same. Not a word was spoken. A moment later I, too, made the sign of the cross. The river and the trees prayed in silence.

The serenity that followed was like a gentle bath.

"Well, Don Oshva, so you've given up the idea of working the mines?" asked the old man, and his words fell pleasantly on our ears.

"*Quién sabe!* Getting machinery up there would be very difficult and would take a lot of money. I think I would do better to pan gold in this river which Don Juan says is very rich."

"Why, Don Oshva, panning any old way we can always get gold when we want it. Not only on the beach but on the farms. . . . It's everywhere."

"Yes, I'm going to examine it and make my analyses. Then I'll go back to Lima and convince the men who can put up the money. We can organize a company to exploit it as it should be, a company we could call, for instance . . . let's say . . . The Golden Serpent. What do you think of it?"

"It sounds good, Don Oshva."

The engineer went on: "We'll call it The Golden Serpent because seen from above, from the Campana Ridge, for instance, the river looks like a great serpent. And as it is so rich, the name is appropriate and suggestive, don't you think? The Golden Serpent! The company would supply machinery, dredges, and we'd work it right. You people would make money selling your produce! Yucca, bananas, and other things, and working as miners. We'd all get very rich. What do you think of it?"

"It sounds good, Don Oshva, unless you mean that people would have to work all the time."

"The Golden Serpent," the engineer repeated, "The Golden Serpent."

The moon had set and everything was in shadow that grew deeper and deeper. It was hard to see the river now and the trees in the valley were only a black blur. A horse neighed somewhere in the distance, the dappled gray, no doubt, and all that was heard after that was the murmur of the river and the leaves, accompanied by the doleful hooting of the owls.

As we were dropping off to sleep under the fluttering

gauze of the breeze we could hear the engineer turning in the darkness, perhaps seeing between his hands the glittering gold dust. He muttered to himself: "The Golden Serpent."

16

The Golden Serpent

When we woke up, at daybreak, Don Osvaldo was
not with us. What could have happened to him? His
blankets were there, carefully folded, evidence of a
planned departure. He must have gone for a walk, taking advantage of the early morning cool. So without giving it any more thought we went off about our business.

The sun was high when I saw the engineer coming
along the path that went past my garden fence. There
had been a great change in Don Osvaldo. Before he
used to stand out in sharp contrast to us and to the landscape. It was not only his new clothes and his shining
outfit; there was something about him that gave him an
air of considering himself above his surroundings. But
not now. He was in keeping with all the rest, and he
even walked a little stooped over and with quick, short
steps. At that moment he seemed like something the valley had taken to itself as part of itself, weaving him
into the landscape and molding him into the earth. I
couldn't tell very well what had happened, but even his
blond beard no longer seemed blond. And although
last night this transformation made me happy, now it
saddened me. I felt as though I had looked into his
future and it was that of a man who died in the middle
of his journey because he did not know just where he

was going and had almost forgotten where he started from.

I was cutting a bunch of bananas. He saw me and came over to give me a hand, and then walked home with me.

He sat down on a little stool that was standing near by and answered briefly in the affirmative when I asked him if he had gone for a walk. Then he became silent and looked as though he were thinking of weighty matters. These must have accompanied him on his walk.

He watched me in silence as I hung up the bunch of bananas on the porch, with many others that were already ripe. His face was pale and his arms hung as though he were fatigued. He still said nothing as he ate the bananas I offered him, and then he asked for water, drinking great swallows of it from the new jug I handed him.

"So long," he said, getting quickly to his feet and starting down the path.

"When are you going to look at the placers?"

"Maybe later on this afternoon."

But he did not set foot out of Don Matías's house that afternoon. Nor the next day. For a whole week he talked about his great enterprise and made plans. At night—so the old man said—he would leave the bunk where he slept on the porch and not come back until morning. But now it seemed that he was really going. He had definitely decided to start the next day and had hired Pablo and Julián to help him.

It was a gay bright morning the engineer had chosen to go off to explore the river. The sun had risen in a brilliant blue sky flecked here and there with a white cloud, and it flooded the valley with light. The birds sang and the river murmured pleasantly as it flowed by. A fresh, fragrant breath rose from the earth, and the trees flaunted their lush exuberance.

The engineer talked enthusiastically as he ate his breakfast, infected by the vigor and brilliance of the April day. His helpers had come and they were ready to leave, when down the street came Hormecinda, driving her goats to the hills.

The girl left her flock and came toward us, greeting us in her bell-like voice, her hat in her hand. Then she called Don Osvaldo to one side and handed him a little package. Her golden face was covered with blushes and tears trembled in her eyes.

In a timid voice she said: "Something for you to eat on the way, sir."

And she trotted quickly off after her herd, taking care that they should not stray into the planted fields. Don Osvaldo stood looking after her for a long time, and when he turned to us again he was intensely pale. His only words were directed to Pablo and Julián.

"Let's go," and his voice choked as he said it.

They picked up their saddlebags and started out. The engineer put the package Hormecinda had given him in his bag, and he walked by us, with a taciturn farewell.

"I'll be seeing you. . . . Thanks a lot."

Afterward the *cholos* told that one of the first nights, when they made camp by the river, Don Osvaldo could not contain himself and said to them: "No matter how hard a man tries to prevent it, there are certain things that touch him. Tell me, do you think Hormecinda loves me?"

They had answered yes, because she had even tried to be of help to him, and Don Osvaldo had not been able to close his eyes the whole night.

Don Osvaldo made his survey quickly. He spent a number of days, upstream, examining the sand and taking samples. The whole area showed good results. In the backwater there was an incredible amount of gold. The deposit probably reached to Pataz and possibly beyond.

One afternoon on their way back to Calemar, when the air felt like molten metal, they stopped on the bank in a grove of *gualangos* to escape the fiery rays of the sun.

They were happy: the *cholos* had their pockets full of *soles* which they had made with very little work; Don Osvaldo, his samples and his very favorable report.

He walked away from them behind some bushes and reappeared as naked as his mother had borne him. He dove into a pool and swam around. The touch of the cool, crystal clear water was like a caress. The *cholos,* seated at the foot of the *gualangos,* looked the other way so as not to embarrass him, and he came out laughing and teasing them about their prudishness. He dressed quickly and, refreshed by his swim, felt completely at peace with the world. He sat down at the foot of a thick *higuerón,* whose huge leaves were like open hands between him and the sun.

The smoke from his cigarette curled upward and disappeared in the bright shimmer of the air, and the only sounds that came to his ears above the whirring of the locusts were the monotonous clack of the lime gourds and the sleepy murmur of the river. The shade was damp and enervating. It was a pleasant moment to dream and plan.

He would go to Lima and start his company. He would make those fortunes sleeping in safety vaults shake off their lethargy and multiply in this magic bed. And Ethel? The recollection of the girl with whom he had cocktails at the Country Club brought him a very special feeling. He remembered as never before how exquisite and beautiful she was, and her kisses tasting of créme de menthe and her fragrance of Coty perfume would be new and sweeter than ever after the coca and the rustic perfumes of these valleys. What a feeling of satin, that of her red lips under his cracked by the wind and the sun! The astonishment in her blue eyes when he related his odyssey through these wild mountains! Yes, he would be rich and they would marry. The delight of clasping in his arms her lithe body between the fragrant sheets in the lovely house they would have there, on the sea, back in civilization once more! Ethel had firm round breasts and a waist as flexible as a willow wand. She would give herself to him in a complete yielding, in a civilized manner, not like these *cholas* whom you have to subjugate like a wild animal, and then, even when they have yielded, it is as though they were not there. As for Hormecinda, there was no need to be sentimental about the matter. She would take up with some *cholo* around there. He would leave for Lima as soon as he reached Calemar, so there would be no time for scenes. After all, tears always upset one. No, he would give her no opportunity to cry in his presence. That was settled: Ethel should be his wife and there would surely be a son and then . . .

But first he had to get his company organized. The Golden Serpent would be a success. He would give those young stay-at-homes of Lima a lesson, always hanging around trying to get a government job, and spending their lives bent over a desk or bowing and scraping to their political chiefs. He could have done like Juan Carlos, who, through pull, was holding down a job in Lima as commissioner of a road which did not exist. But no, never, he would be the leader of crusade in favor of a full, virile life, with the gleam of the sun on a man's forehead and the gleam of gold between his fingers. The Golden Serpent!

But after all these fine projects, an uneasiness came over him which he was at a loss to explain. What was it? And he began to think about himself, how much he had changed, chewing coca, sleeping with the *cholos,* going through suffering with rare endurance, and even believing in ghost stories. He saw that he was no longer the man from Lima he had once been, but neither was he a man of the Marañón. Other doubts rose to gnaw at his vitals. Would he come back? Would he go? Everything that surrounded him was awesome, overwhelming and he himself didn't even know the mental and physical chasms he had crossed, nor those that might yet wait for him. And then he realized that man counts for little in these worlds, and he said to himself, in a low voice: "Here Fate is Nature."

The sun had set and they had to go on. It was only four hours to Calemar. The young man sat up, and called to the Indians: "Hey . . ."

That was as far as he got for he gave a jump as he felt a sharp bite on his neck. He turned as something whipped against his shoulder and he caught a glimpse of a slender, lithe yellow snake which had jumped into the *higuerón* and was lost from sight as it glided swiftly from branch to branch, losing itself in the thick foliage. It gleamed like a ribbon of gold against the leaves.

Don Osvaldo screamed, calling the *cholos* who came rushing up.

"A snake . . . a yellow snake," he told them, "it went that way."

His trembling hand pointed to the branches. The *cholos* looked up into the dense foliage without making any effort to find it for they knew it would be useless.

"It's a viper, señorito, the *intiwaraka.*"

The engineer fell into silent despair. If ever a man feels alone and helpless it is when a stealthy viper bites him in one of those out-of-the-way ravines of the Marañón. How can he help himself? The presence of other people is useless, too. The only thing that is certain is the loneliness of the poisoned, dying body. A growing burning sensation spread from his neck to his back. The *cholos* did not know what to do: they had no lemons, no red-hot irons, no burning brands. Perhaps cutting the wound . . . but their knives were very dull.

"Your knife, sir."

The engineer dazedly felt through all his pockets and finally pulled one out. Pablo took it and two deep slashes made the sign of a cross at the point of the wound. The blood flowed out freely under the pressure of the heavy hands of the *cholos,* but Don Osvaldo felt that his feet were going to sleep, and neither his arms, his legs, nor even his thorax responded with the suffering of a live thing to his anguished pinches.

Within him threshed the viper of despair. What could be more stupid than to finish his life like this, forgotten and alone, in a wretched savage world? Yes, wretched and savage in the midst of its far-flung gold. What could be done to save him? What? He did not know what to do with his limp hands and his feet were so numb they could no longer hold him up.

He slipped to the ground trembling, while a cold sweat ran in sticky drops down his pale, drawn face. Shadows began to float before his eyes. The *cholos* looked on in silence: Pablo cleaning off the thin blade of the blood-covered knife, Julián chewing his coca and moving his lime gourd. They knew that any aid they might get would be too late, and they stolidly awaited the young man's death. He was as pale as though he were already dead, but he breathed heavily, and his limbs quivered and writhed. Suddenly he grew stiff. His mouth contracted for one last time and his eyes dilated as though they were about to burst from their sockets, trying to see through the shadows thickening about them. The rise and fall of his chest grew slower. At last his eyes closed in defeat. Slowly, while death still croaked in his vitals, his eyelids came together like doors that were closed forever.

"Is he dead?"

"Poor fellow, he's dead now."

Julián and Pablo brought him to Calemar on a litter of poles covered with branches. His body had turned black. The next day, after watching beside him all night, we buried him.

The Golden Serpent!

17

Coca

In front of my cabin the wind rustled through the field of coca. The bushes swayed showing the top and the underside of their leaves in great waves. It was an unending play of pale green and dark green, whose rise and fall finally made my head swim as I sat hunched over on a stone, watching the sunset. An intense odor enveloped me. It was the coca of the other planters that was drying in the reed baskets. It was picking time, but I had not decided to start yet. My hands trembled and a mortal uneasiness ran through my body.

And there was my field of coca, swaying, swaying in the face of my unhappiness, swaying as if it wanted to tell me something. The berries attracted the turtledoves, and they came pecking at the little red fruits and singing the same song my heart would sing. I did not know if that melancholy song came from my breast or entered into it, whether it was the turtledoves' or mine, but it was one and the same. Once I had been the first to pick my coca, to dry it and then pack it in baskets to load it on the donkey's back and go out among the villages to sell it. But now I was dull and my will power was gone, and if the swaying of the plants distressed me and the mournful song of the doves seemed my own, there was something that upset me more than all this: the coca I chewed and chewed and which always tasted bitter to me.

It has been like this since a good or ill-gotten day. Like this.

Florinda had been unhappy for a long time. Then she began to sing again and it was I who heard her first song.

One morning I was up where the reed grass grows beside the river, at the foot of the cliff where the valley begins, to cut some reeds for some panpipes and I heard a clear song that spread out like a bright light of the sun. I liked it, and I trailed it, like a dog its master, to see who was singing. It was Florinda, who after finishing her washing had undressed and was bathing in the river. The shirts, spread out over the reeds, were yawning their damp breath.

Florinda was like a cedar carved in the form of a woman. In the near-by fields the fruits on the heavy-laden trees were swaying back and forth gently. Florinda went on with her song and it seemed to me that she would be singing in my heart forever; a song of rock and living water. A song of the river.

The Marañón reflected over her young graceful body the blue of its immensity. The wind blew and the reeds were like a panpipe played by a thousand voices. Florinda stood there, naked, while nature surrounded her with a gesture of admiration. Even the rough cliffs seemed to sharpen their edges the better to see her. Her flesh was the color of terra cotta. Her limbs were strong, her belly a gentle curve and her undefiled breasts were terse with their life-giving promise beneath the radiant smile of her full lips. Her big hazel eyes, encircled by bluish shadows, characteristic of the women of these valleys, idly watched her agile hands splashing and playing in the transparent May water.

I slipped slowly toward her through the reeds.

"Florinda," I called to her in a voice I had never heard before.

With a start of fright she made for the bank covering herself with her clothes as best she could. I cannot say what the look she gave me was like: that of a dove, an owl, or a viper. I was making my way toward her crouched like a puma when someone shouted: "Florindaaa!"

I ran downstream through the reed bed, came out the other side, and began to slash furiously at the reeds with my machete. Every stroke of the swift knife cut down a sheaf of them. It was her father, Don Pancho, who was coming with a bundle in his hand.

"Have you seen Florinda around here?"

"Someone's singing over there."

"Her mother wants her to wash this, too."

"She must be over that way."

"And what are you doing here?" asked the old man, whetting a suspicion on the swift gleam of his alert little eyes.

"I came down to cut reed to see if I could make some panpipes. . . . The fellows at Bambamarca always want them."

"M-hm, all right, man."

Don Pancho walked off whistling and tripping over the roots of the reeds.

Ever since that day I was I, and yet I was another. I felt so lonely in my cabin. I chewed coca without stopping and it always tasted bitter to me. Was Florinda really afraid? Wasn't she just surprised? Or did she get mad? Coca, the great assuager of sorrow, made me feel sad, and a choking fear had taken possession of my flesh and my soul. Doña Mariana said I "must have caught a chill," and I couldn't talk the way I did before with the Romeros and the other *cholos*. I existed only for myself and yet not really even for myself: for nobody.

At night the hooting of the owls frightened me. Is it true that they foretell death? Of course we have to die, but not because of their call, if that were true there'd be nobody alive in our valley. But not even this logical reasoning helped me. When they began the doleful chant of their hooting in the darkness, I wished that I were not alone. From the bowels of the shadows tragic portents reared themselves against me and the owl gave me warning of them. No, I wished that I were not alone.

And the coca was bitter, always bitter.

At times I thought perhaps the morning, with its radiant light and the twittering of its joyous birds would bring back peace to me, and the old happiness would surge through my veins. The joy of being alive, of sowing and harvesting, of crossing the river now and again, of hearing the vast murmuring of the forest and the endless flowing of the waters. . . . But the coca was bitter to my tongue and the coca never lied. Something unlucky had crossed my path.

But perhaps not. What is there the soothsaying coca does not know? My coca was merely making me be on guard every moment, scan life deeply, look for clues that might elude me. The leaf was wise, and perhaps it would have good news for me some day and I would find my happiness again.

And so I thought about my coca, questioning my bitter coca, asking counsel from it and hoping that it would once more sweeten my mouth with that sweetness that was in itself a miracle.

One night I planned to go out. To go toward someone. Was it toward Florinda? Yes, the coca would lead me to Florinda. I had spied on her many times but she never went far from her house by herself. Now the only thing I wanted was to go where she was and carry her off, have her in the middle of the fields, and then die. People would say that Lucas Vilca went crazy, but I didn't care. The coca was bitter in my mouth.

"I am going. Coca, kill me or give her to me. Be my guide."

I went out and looked around on all sides without seeing anything but the black night. One tiny star winked high, high in the sky and I started walking without knowing where I was going. Florinda! Florinda! The coca was bitter. Branches scratched my face. Owl, go on hooting for now your warning is not in vain. This was the reed bed because it sounded like panpipes in the wind. And here was the river. And this was the place. And here was where Florinda stood, hiding her body from my eager eyes. And there she was, too, naked amidst these waters that barely showed a ripple on their black waves.

"Why don't you speak to me, coca?"

My tongue pressed a long time against the damp bitter wad.

"Don't refuse her to me, leaf of my ancestors. Don't be bitter under my tongue. Speak sweetly to me, with the sweetness of the honeycomb and the ripe fruits. My father said that you showed his father the future; why not to me, then, who asks you from morning to night and from night to morning, and who never wearies of waiting? Or is it that you have already answered with your bitterness and am I disobeying you by insisting? But I do not want to spit you from my mouth, doubtless because you don't want me to. . . ."

So I prayed beside the river. So I prayed to the coca for a long time.

Suddenly the tip of my tongue grew numb and there was the taste of honey on it and my nerves quivered at receiving the message. Now what was that which emerged from the waters, and came to rest among them like a corpse and yet flowed with light? It rose, it stood erect, the water reaching halfway up its thighs. It was Florinda! There she stood with her high breasts and her moist mouth and her great hazel eyes, in a halo of light. I rushed toward her where. she was trustingly playing with the water, but I fell down and I felt an intense cold pierce through my ears to my brain. When I got up, Florinda was no longer there. She had gone, the river had taken her from me because the river is an outlaw. Florinda! Florinda! But the anguish had gone from my heart and I calmly crawled out of the river, my nerves settled and the fire of my flesh died down.

The coca had grown sweet to make me see Florinda, and the river had taken her from me. Yes, the coca had given her to me. I could rest easily. It had brought me peace. She would come to me some day to yield me her body like a virgin field.

In my cabin I kept on chewing and the sound of the

owls was now like the song of the rain to me. My mouth had grown numb, and a subtle sweetness penetrated my brain and my heart, my blood and my bones. My coca had become sweet and something good was going to happen to me. I sank into sleep, sleep. . . .

A *quiénquién* awakened me with its shrill question as the sun was falling straight above the little patio. A yellow and black bird was in the house pecking at something in a saddlebag hanging from the reed wall.

"Get out, you nuisance."

The bird got out through the wall and flew away. I got up and saw that today was like any other day. Here was my house, there my field, this was Calemar, that was the river, just like any other day, as it was in the beginning and ever shall be. My sorrow had departed and I felt almost as though it had never existed. My tongue still tasted the same delicate sweetness that had been there all night in that well-chewed ball, with its knowledge of good and evil.

I stepped out to take a look at the fences, something I had not done for long time. The birds were singing their heads off. The fence needed mending. The coca leaves had grown larger and thicker, bigger and better, and the harvest was going to be good. And look at the way the bananas had grown!

Suddenly I saw Florinda coming down the path that wound between the bushes and pasture lots beside the fence. I started toward my cabin and we both got there at the same time. Her hands played with the glossy braids that rose and fell over her breasts.

"My father says have you got any chile . . . ?"

"Certainly, Flori, of course I have."

She watched me as I threw the basket that was lying in the corner into the middle of the room. Her eyes followed every movement I made, and I took my time untying the rope with which it was tied. "She's not mad," I thought. "The coca has tasted sweet ever since last night." The coca gave me courage.

"Tell me," I asked, as I chewed the wise leaves, "do you still think about Roge?"

"Oh, poor fellow, but he's dead now." The chile shone bright in the top of the basket.

"Come and get it."

She held out her full percale skirt, showing her neat ankles.

"You know I love you very much, really I do."

"Now if you're going to start telling lies, Don Lusha . . ."

"Lusha? Why do you call me that?"

Her eyes and her smile yielded to me.

"I think it sounds prettier than just to say Lucas."

"That's fine if you only loved me."

She let her skirt go and began to tremble. I put my hands on her hips and my breath came panting, as I drew her to me. Her back curved under my desire.

We were lost in the deep forest of limbs and muscles on fire, of sweetness and complaint, of choking and anguish, where roots as old as man himself penetrate and are nourished with blood.

Afterwards she told me—and all the time I kept thinking of the blessed coca leaves—that last night she had dreamed about me and we were down by the river.

I took the chile to her house and one afternoon, after I had talked with her father, we came back to my house together. That is how Florinda became my wife.

It was the coca that gave her to me.

18

The Outlaw

Like the water of the river he was never quiet. He came and went. One moment he was going up the canyon, and the next he was coming down. How far? How long? He could never answer. Chance ruled his life, and so time and distance did not exist for him. He traveled even when he was at rest, because if he stopped it was only to get ready and start off again.

And he was a human being like all of us, like you, like me. Except that he was an outlaw. The law was after him and he would have let himself die by inches rather than allow himself to be caught and brought to town, where they would let him rot like a worthless piece of trash in the corner of some prison while on some desk a stack of official papers about him would pile up. When the folder of legal documents was considered sufficient, he would be taken from the capital of the department to Lima, to that famous city which is known to us for two reasons: it's there they change the government and it's there they have the biggest jail. It's easy enough to get into it but very few ever get out. And what is the difference between twenty years or more in jail and death? Even after he has served his sentence, the man will always be a prisoner, for on his eyes will be tattooed the bars that imprisoned his soul, and mortified his flesh, and destroyed his nerves and rotted his bones.

So the outlaw knew what he was doing when he clung to his restless life. The river gorge was his land and his home. It protected him and fed him. It also comforted him and strengthened him. That abrupt sweep of hard rocks, echoing the sound of the river, cool with trees, burning with sun, was harsh and made a man strong, molding him in its own image, and at the same time caressing him with its warm strength.

One night a horse stopped in front of my house and someone alighted and knocked at my door.

"Hey, Cayetano."

My father had been dead these many years, and here was someone who thought he was alive. Who could it be? He spoke with a deep clear voice.

"Ña Meche," he then called.

"Just a minute, man," I answered, getting up.

When I opened the door there stood a man I could not recognize, neither his stocky silhouette, nor his features, veiled by the darkness.

"Is Cayo or Ña Meche here?"

"No, they died a long time ago. I am their son, Lucas."

He laid a thick, heavy hand upon my shoulder. There was something cordial and affectionate in his touch.

"I knew you when you were just a little tad. You didn't have good sense yet. And now you're a man . . . Can you put me up here?"

"Of course."

"All right, then, I'm going to turn my horse loose. Is the barn lot still over on that side where it used to be?"

"Yes, there it is."

The man quickly unsaddled his horse and led it away. In the meantime Florinda started a fire to fix him something to eat. When he came back we sat down around the fire.

His was a hard face as though hewn out of rock with a few blows of a sledge hammer. His sparse, bristly beard did not hide the firm line of his jaw. In his calm and steady eyes there was a melancholy but determined look. A grizzled lock hung over his forehead beneath a dark, torn palm-leaf hat. His ear must have been on the alert every minute, for the noise Florinda made breaking a stick over her knees made him whirl quickly around. When he realized what it was a faint smile appeared on his dark, firmly set lips.

Afterwards he said: "You know, lad, that I'm in trouble with the law."

"For a long time?"

"A long time, I don't even remember how long now. More than twenty . . ."

"Years?"

"Yes."

Then he pulled out of his pocket a bundle wrapped up in a red bandanna, and opened it, revealing the dark lead and yellow brass of revolver bullets.

"You got a little grease?" he asked Florinda.

And he rubbed the bullets one by one against the roll of fat.

"They are my defense. Without them, what would become of me? The poor man is respected only when he can kill."

He completed his task quickly in spite of the size of his gnarled hands.

"And why have you been on the outs with the law for so long?"

"It's a long story. I'm from here, from Calemar, though I expect it's only the old folks who remember me now. The first thing that went wrong was in town, where a feast was being held. I went there to sell my coca and, as it happened, the big day of the feast I had had a couple of drinks. And there was a group of big shots there, mounted on fine horses. One of them was riding a fiery animal, and without the least considera- tion for the people who were walking through the streets, he rode me down. I got up and told him what

I thought of him, and he got mad and whirled his horse at me again, and rode me down a second time. This time when I got up I didn't say a word to him but gave him such a slash in the belly that first his guts fell out and then he came tumbling down after them. It turned out that he was a rancher, and the law got after me so hard I had to take flight. I left here. If it had been some sort of trouble among poor folks, they'd have forgotten about it, and nothing would have come of it, but as it was a gentleman who had been killed, they never let up. And time went by and I was still an outlaw when a group came after me to take me, and I was galloping down a mountainside for they had me surrounded. Someone they called a lieutenant thought he had me and he was taking aim when I beat him to the draw and left him as dead as a doornail. From then on things have got worse. I have just come from Jecumbuy, for I had a feeling that they were on my trail."

He finished his job and handed back the rest of the grease.

"There's always some rascal ready to turn me in. I haven't had any luck. I settle down and get a piece of land to cultivate, when all of a sudden they get wind of me and I have to start my wanderings again. And in all these troubles others have died, too. So even if the killing of the rancher ever became outlawed, there'd still be the lieutenant and the others. And now they even blame me for killings I haven't done. When anybody is killed anywhere around the police say: 'That's some more of Riero's work.' To hear them tell it, I don't know how many I have killed. Patience..."

He helped himself to his food with evident enjoyment.

"Ah, my lad, if you knew how good a gourdful of something hot tastes to an outlaw. Day after day on parched corn. There was a time when I had nothing to eat but custard apples, when I was way up in the ravines. . . ."

"And when will all the charges against you be outlawed?"

"*Quién sabe?* With all the murders they have laid at my door, I don't see when. . . . Maybe never . . . They call me a terrible murderer, but, as far as my conscience is concerned, I have killed only that rancher, and the lieutenant and two other troopers who tried to catch me, all in self-defense."

"Yes, the name of Riero is well known."

"You see even I don't know how many people I am supposed to have killed."

His mouth twisted in a wry smile.

"And where are you going now?"

"Up in the hills. But it's better for you not to say anything about it. I've been traveling around a lot. I am at home near the river, like a good valley man. I told you that I am from here and I want you to know that I was a good friend to your father. All the way down to the port of Balsas, I know the country upstream and down almost as far as Huanuco. I would have found a place for myself somewhere, but I've had no luck. After all, this canyon is a good place to hide. If they come down on one side I can cross to the other, horse and all. Or if not, I can ride down the cliffs. The river is always good."

After he had finished eating, the outlaw made up his bed on the porch, using his blankets and the pallets from his horse. To let him get his rest we stopped talking and went into the cabin. In a little while we heard his deep, regular breathing and knew he was asleep.

Very early in the morning, while it was still dark, he called in to say good-bye.

"Well, boy," he said curtly but sincerely, "my name is Ignacio Ramos and you know they call me Riero. It's far better for you not to say anything about my being here, because everywhere there are wagging tongues. All there is for me to do now is to go, and keep going always, without stopping. If you should ever be in trouble with the law, maybe I can be of help to you some way."

And just as he mounted and was ready to ride off, he said: "If a fellow by the name of Ramón Jara, nicknamed Pepe should come this way, give him lodging. I'm going to tell him to come here."

And he touched the spurs to his horse, who reared back on his hind legs before starting off at a gallop. It was dawn but it seemed to me that for this man the day would never come. That he would always be in darkness, in an endless night of flight and fear. . . . Still, it would be a night without walls and iron bars, night with freedom, night with stars overhead.

19

We Stay Because We Are Men

Yesterday, like today, like tomorrow, the river roars and breaks against the cliff upstream at the head of the valley that protects Calemar. The cliff stands firm and our land holds fast. But we *cholos* belong to the river more than to the land and "we stay because we are men and we have to live on the terms life offers."

Cattle buyers came by. They grew more numerous every year, and had already driven to the coast all the cattle from the other side of the river. For the moment they had passed us by. Not a corner, however remote and dangerous, would escape their search. Not a single animal, no matter how stunted or poor, would they miss. Don Policarpio Núñez and his son came through, their Winchesters across their saddle stocks, on their way to Marcapata, Bambamarca, Shomenate, El Olivo, Cionera. They were going to drive down all the cattle from those parts.

"Don Juan Plaza has stock to sell," remarked old Matías.

"So have the Indians," answered Don Policarpio, jingling the *soles* in his vest pocket. Don Policarpio had money and his saddlebags were surely full of bills. Across the broad span of his stomach hung a thick gold chain which passed through a button of his vest. The Winchesters looked after everything, but Don Policarpio probably used his carbine in matters that had nothing to do with self-defense.

"You folks will get my cattle across, I take it?" the trader went on, looking at us one by one with his sly little eyes and smiling blandly all over his fat jowls and his puffy dark cheeks.

"Certainly, we'll take them across."

But the raft Arturo brought up was not large enough and we went for another. In La Escalera, where the water was low enough so we could see the bristling jagged rocks, we thought of poor Roge, and plied our paddles furiously. Arturo's jaws were set until the dark skin was drawn tight over the tendons. His face was like the rapids itself, sullen and threatening. We reached the spot about noon, for we had started early, so the sun would be high and light the place well. We had to get through. It was not fitting that the river should trifle with us, first-class ferrymen that we were. The river made its rapids and inflowing currents spin about in a way to make your head swim, and held its sharp rocks to the breast like daggers, but our eyes were quick to see the way between the ridges, our arms stronger than ever to handle the paddles through the voracious waters. We were nothing but arms and eyes. We did not even notice the roaring of the rapids, and it was only when we had turned the corner and the raft had come out on the quiet waters that we heard it muttering oaths at our backs. It was threatening us about the next time, which might—who knows—be the the last time. "As many times as you like," replied as one our jubilant loud-beating hearts.

We had agreed with old Matías that he was to meet us, and he had been waiting for three hours on the bank. When he saw us he trembled with joy, and his face was one broad smile.

"Good, lads, good. The river can't frighten men like you."

We were never so happy to be together as that night, and the warmth we felt came, not from the valley, but from our own hearts. We gathered in a ring around the table, where the coca was heaped in a thick pile: Don Matías and his son, Silverio and Encarna, our companions of the raft, Jacinto and Santos, and several more *cholos* who had come to celebrate our "happy landing."

A jug of rum passed from hand to hand around the circle, and the bright gleam of the fire lighted up our faces in the midst of the black night.

The rum quickly set our blood on fire and then we laughed heartily over the incidents of the trip and the gay gossip of Shicún, but after a while the coca reached our hearts so that once again we might feel the sadness that lies beneath the surface of our lives, always quick to raise its head and show itself.

The rushing of the river and the hooting of the owls was our only link with reality. Otherwise it would have seemed at first glance that this group of men was the creation of a gleam of light in a thick sinister world of shadows.

Arturo told how in Shicún a *cholo* who had been in the habit of setting nets in a branch of the river went to look at them one afternoon and never came back again. His relatives looked for him for several days down the river. On the broad banks where corpses are generally washed up, they found nothing. At the same time, though they did not know for sure whether he had been drowned or not, nobody doubted that he was dead.

"Perhaps he went to some other place," remarked a *cholo*.

"No, he left all his things behind—there they were. And he said as he always did that he'd be back right away and he didn't come. He even left his poncho. He certainly must have died."

Old Matías spoke up then, slowly, as though he were tasting and weighing his words: "Oh, what a changeable river. You can't exactly say that it isn't good, but pure goodness is not to be found in this world. Don Oshva knew what he was saying, although he was talking about it from a different point of view, when he called this river a golden serpent. That's right: a serpent of gold it is."

The old man fell silent, and none of his listeners said a word. Perhaps he felt that we had not completely grasped his idea, and went on: "Look how well all of us live here. We want for nothing and it is all thanks to the river. This valley belongs to it, the water we row across belongs to it. It never stops flowing and the only bad thing about it is the danger . . . but it comes when we least expect it, and the beautiful river kills us in its own beautiful valleys, and it kills us suddenly, like a golden sepent."

"That's the God's truth, Don Matish."

"That's certainly true."

The old man kept on talking. His little eyes twinkled brightly under the drooping brim of his hat. Although they seemed fixed on us, it was as though he did not see us. His look went much farther.

"A gentleman told me that in the olden times the Peruvians adored the river and the serpent, too, like gods. And I'm thinking maybe they did this because there's not much difference between them, and as they didn't know which of the two was more important, they worshipped them both. . . ."

In silence we added coca to the wads we were chewing. We were careful not to rattle the lime gourds so as to make no noise.

"So there you are," went on the old man, "our river flows everlastingly on, and at times we curse it from the bottom of our hearts, but it looks as though it just laughed at us. . . . Yet do we run away from it? No, because we are men and you have to take life as it comes and for us our life is the river. So, up and at it, boys. And we must never let discouragement get the better of us. Do you know how the Devil spread evil through the world?"

"I do," said Arturo, "but maybe the rest don't."

"Tell it, tell it, Don Matish," clamored several voices.

"Then I'll tell you, and don't forget it, because it's something a Christian should always bear in mind."

And he told us the story we will never forget and which we will tell our children, entrusting it to them to tell their children, and so it will be handed down from one generation to the other and it will never be lost.

"Once upon a time the Devil set out to sell evil through the world. Man had sinned and he was already damned, but there wasn't any variety of evils. It was then that the Devil set out with his pack on his back, and he traveled all the paths of the world selling the evils he had wrapped up in packages in his pack, for he had made them into powders. There were powders of all colors, poverty and sickness, avarice and hate and wealth which is also an evil, and ambition, which is an evil, too, when it goes beyond a certain limit. . . . Not one single evil had been left out. And among those packages there was a little white one and that was to make you lose heart.

"And so people bought things from him, and they all bought sickness, and poverty and avarice, and the more thoughtful ones bought wealth and ambition. And it was all to spread evil among Christians. And the Devil sold them at a good price. They looked at the little white package but nobody paid much attention to it. 'Now what would this be,' they asked just out of curiosity. And the Devil answered: 'Discouragement,' and they said 'that's not very much of an evil,' and nobody bought it. And the Devil got mad because he thought the people were too stupid. And when, out of idle curiosity or because someone wanted it just for a whim, they asked 'how much,' the Devil answered 'so much.' And it was such a big price that he asked, more than for any of the others, that the people began to laugh. They said that as the package was so little and the evil itself wasn't very big it wasn't right for him to ask such a price, and they began to insult the Devil, saying he was a terrible Devil to try to cheat them. And that made the Devil real mad, and he began to laugh, too, at seeing how stupid people were.

"And that is how he sold all the evils but nobody wanted to buy the little package because it was so small, and besides discouragement wasn't such a great evil. Then the Devil said. 'If you buy this one, I'll sell you the others; otherwise, not a one.' And the people looked at one another, laughing heartily, for it seemed as if the Devil had suddenly become addlepated. And there lay the last little package and nobody would give a penny for it. Then the devil, madder than ever, laughed as only the Devil can laugh, and said: 'We'll see who takes the last trick!' and he scattered the powder in the wind so it would be carried over the whole world.

"And when he did this all the other evils went, too, because this evil is part of all them. You only have to think it over to realize this. If you are rich and lucky and discouragement gets its claws into you, nothing seems worthwhile and vice becomes your master. . . . If you are poor and lowly, then discouragement makes you still worse off. And that is how the Devil sowed evil throughout the world, for without loss of heart not a single evil could harm anybody.

"So there is discouragement, all over the world. It always comes, to some more, to others less. And nobody can be really good because he cannot endure as he should the terrible struggle between body and soul which is life.

"Christians of Calemar: never let discouragement take hold of our hearts. . . ."

One day the hillside became a mass of colors and shouts.

Don Policarpio Núñez and his son, with three Indian herders they had hired, came down driving a herd of a hundred wild cattle. The herd would not stay in the road but kept trying to take refuge in the chamiso thickets, the cactus and the ravine, trying to break away from the roundup and get back to their old stamping grounds. But the herders sought them out in their hiding places or, from the buttes or rocks, whirling the dark circles of their slings through the air, let fly at them with stones, making them turn back with big bruises on their sides and join the others in the road.

As they came down the narrow pathway they used the goad on them to make those poor scrubby cattle of the highlands swim across the river.

From their saddles Don Policarpio and his son cracked their bull whips over the herd, and the herders slung stones at the heads of the leaders. The straps of their slings gave a loud snap with each shot. They were trying to keep the cattle from drinking when they reached the river, for, if they do, it is impossible to get them across. The herd galloped down the road closing in until they formed a multicolored mass in the cloud of dust they raised.

The one in front, taken by surprise and pushed on by the others, had no choice but to throw herself into the river and about twenty followed her. Animals who had never known what a river was swam like our dead Roge.

The others stayed on the bank greedily plunging their muzzles into the stream, paying no attention to the whip lashes, stones, and cries that rained upon them. They withstood them steadfastly, and went on drinking or jumping about among the rocks to get out of the way of the quirts that laid open their flanks, but still taking a swallow here and there.

Only the heads and horns of those that were swimming showed above the water, like a parenthesis on the rippling surface of the river. The blotch of them narrowed down until it formed a straight line which we of the valley who had gone down to see what was happening watched with interest. So did the owners and the herders, who had stopped goading on the stragglers.

The pitiful herd struggled desperately. Alongside their bodies a white foam began to show, growing wider as it floated downstream. The river began to drag one of the animals under. It was swimming slower, more weakly, and its muzzle was barely visible above the water. At times it seemed as though the river were about to engulf it. It fell out of line. The river had won. . . .

Don Policarpio got more and more exasperated with the poor animal and his puffy face turned purple.

"You good-for-nothing cow," he screamed at it, "why did you jump in the water if you couldn't swim?" And then to his son: "I told you that bag of bones wasn't worth twenty *soles*." The herd kept on battling the water desperately. Their horns looked thinner and they seemed to be making less of an effort, but we realized that it was really greater because they were tiring. Finally the first one reached the bank, and, after slipping a number of times, managed to climb out. Once on the bank, she gave herself a good shake, and then turned toward the ones who were still swimming, giving a long, mournful bellow.

When they heard her, those who were near the bank and the others farther away, quickened their pace. Even the one who had weakened, and was far back and drifting downstream, took heart and swam with her head high out of the water, making a supreme effort to save herself. But her strength failed her, the river took a firmer grip on her and the current glutted its fury on her weakness and discouragement.

All the cows on our side began to low, and in a little while all those who had crossed to the other bank, their eyes fixed on the one that was drowning, took up the sound, in a wild, doleful chorus that seemed to echo endlessly through the cliffs.

Whereupon Don Policarpio—who would have thought it of him!—got off his horse and, kneeling on the ground, pulled back the bolt of his Winchester. He fired four shots, one after the other, at the poor animal. They echoed lugubriously through the canyon, and the lowing of the cows seemed the lament of nature. The river flowed placidly on, in gentle waves, chattering in the low voice it uses in the summer.

The poor cow disappeared in the distance.

Don Policarpio remarked: "Damn it. That's what I call throwing money in the water."

Then he ordered the herders to keep a close watch on those on this side of the river, for those on the other side were pretty well worn out, and would not feel like wandering very far.

All night long in the reed beds along the beach there were bellowings, snortings, shouts, and the whizzing of slings. The cows were trying to turn back. They became enraged and fought so that in the morning they were all panting and their flanks were bleeding. The bats, too, had not been idle. They had bitten them on the loins and two red streaks flowed down the sides of the animals from which they had been sucking blood. Their sorrowful, watery glances were battered back by the sharp cliffs and they could hardly make out the tiny, whitish winding trail that climbed by leaps and bounds toward their beloved highland grazing grounds. They drew back as they looked at the river, trembling with fear.

As soon as it was light we began ferrying them across.

We divided up into squads, one for each raft, and the others to rope the cows and get them aboard. The owners and herders helped with this. What a tussle those wild cows, in no way belying their bringing up in the highlands or the thick underbrush around Cionera, gave us! We had to rope them at a distance, and over and over again, for they defended themselves by lowering their horns as soon as we whirled a rope at them.

We had to drag them to the river, and once we got them to the water and gave them a good push, they were easy to manage. They do not weigh in the water and towing them along was just a matter of skill. Some of them did not want to swim, and would roll over on their sides. But all we had to do was pull them over where we could get hold of them by the horns, and push their heads under water. In a second they were pawing about and came up swimming. At times they even helped the raft to advance.

The real job was to get the rope off them. The *cholos* on the other side led them to a tree, and using this as a parapet, slowly stretched out their hands feeling for the ring of the lasso. But, at the least noise, the cow would attempt to hook the man, or jump back, and whirling swiftly around, charge him. One managed to horn Encarna in the breast, and would have killed him if the *cholo* had not knocked her down with a stone in the forehead. She lay there for a long time kicking her legs around. When she got up, she seemed stunned and walked about shaking her head, her legs buckling under her.

We brought Encarna back to our side of the river and replaced him with Pablo. The wounded *cholo* left a trail of blood on the raft and on the path to his house. If he had had his way Don Policarpio would have put a bullet through every last one of those cows.

But you can't help feeling sorry for the poor animals. Anyone who is attached to his own haunts can imagine what it would be if he were taken to the other side of a river which often takes away the hope of ever returning. The poor cows who first refused to have their horns imprisoned by the lasso, and then to have them freed, lost all their wildness in no time. They stood about under the shade of a *pate* tree, looking sadly at the road down which they must travel, nibbling occasionally at a chamiso twig, while their tails slapped at the mosquitoes gorged with blood on their udders. It was as though they felt that their struggle with man was useless, and even more useless the struggle with the river. That rough, roaring swath, whose bottom their hoofs could not reach, spread a boundless desolation between them and their longing for home.

The job took us two days. Don Policarpio paid us the fifty *soles* we had agreed upon and we returned while he went on, with his son and the herders, driving a long obedient chain, black, red, white, yellow. . . .

There is never a lack of cattle to carry across, nor people: ranchers from our side, peddlers from Celendín, community Indians, tenant farmers. We are always ready, paddle in hand and the rafts under our knees, upon the waves that the Marañón incessantly rolls along.

Five seasons have passed. What is there to tell? Well, for instance . . . But the one who acts and does not tell is our Marañón. They say that fifty leagues upstream it ate away the side of a valley, causing it to slide down, then dug itself a deep channel through the landslide, changed its course and carried away the whole valley. That must have been what happened, because coca plants came floating down mixed with the logs, and a dead man, who was naked because the stream strips the clothes off people. The water was muddier than we had ever seen it, black, the color of night. We did not see any more dead. All we know for certain is that the Chusgón, a tributary of the Marañón that flows into it about three leagues below our land, washed away almost the whole valley of Shimbuy, dragging the fields of coca into the river. There is nothing our Marañón won't do.

Five years have passed and many more will follow. We will probably die without remembering how many there were. Life is like the river for those who live beside it: always the same and always different. And in a rhythm of rising and falling waters, there we are, the boatmen, steadfastly crossing the river, joining the regions it separates, binding them together.

Don Matías is now very old, and death will soon call for him, the same as the other veteran boatmen: old Cunshe, Don Crisanto, Encarna himself, who is already stooped over, as when a man gets tired rowing. The years are like a slow whirlpool which grows deeper, dragging people into it.

But here we are, and when our last hour comes— on land or water, it doesn't matter—there will be Adán and all the other little *cholos* who already know how to handle a paddle. There will be no lack of boatmen. Lucinda and Florinda and all the other women in the valley will always keep us supplied. Hormecinda looks after a fair-haired little son, who cannot call to his father, but to whom the rafts already call.

Besides Roge and Don Osvaldo, many others have died. During our festivals, between drink after drink and dance after dance, we say a prayer for them. That's all. Nobody can spend his life weeping and praying over the dead. In the struggle with the river, life is danger and we give death the place it deserves. Not for nothing does the old song ring on our lips:

> "River Marañón, let me cross.
> You are strong and powerful.
> You never forgive.
> River Marañón, I have to cross.
> You have your waters,
> I, my heart."

And the river hears us and goes murmuring on, calm in summer, wild and overpowering in the rainy season. Then a raft is our very heart bursting with courage. We were born here and we feel in our veins the powerful, magnificent surge of the earth. In the forest the wind intones a hymn to the abundance of life. The river roars at our determination to live. The banana trees hang down their thick swaying clusters, and the fruits of the alligator pears and *lucumas* swell like turgid breasts. The oranges roll their golden balls upon the ground, and the coca is bitter and sweet like our story.

The cliffs—landmarks of the earth—rise to heaven to point out to the Christians of this valley where life is really life.

Afterword

The real protagonist of this novel is the Marañón River, the "Golden Serpent." Rising high in the mountains of Peru it flows northeastward, its waters increased by many tributaries, into Brazil, where it is joined by other rivers from the northern watershed to form the mightiest river of them all, the Amazon, "Mother of Waters."

Of the many brave men who have measured their strength against that of the river, history records the names of two: Francisco de Orellana and Lope de Aguirre. Both had shared in the conquest of Peru with Francisco Pizarro. Orellana, who founded the city of Guayaquil, in 1541 joined the expedition his distant relative, Gonzalo Pizarro, half-brother of Francisco, had organized to go in search of the fabled kingdom of El Dorado and the reported cinnamon groves. Few expeditions were ever prepared with more care and forethought, but, nevertheless, it quickly ran into trouble. Most of the Indians who had been recruited for the undertaking in Quito sickened or died as the party descended into the tropical lowlands, as did a number of the Spaniards; the densely wooded terrain made the use of the horses impossible; and the party's abundant supplies were rapidly becoming depleted. In view of all this it was decided to build a boat and sail down the river they had been following in the hope of finding the rich lands the Indians they encountered told them about—probably to get rid of them—where there would be food. Out of trees they chopped down, nails hammered from the horses' shoes, sails and rigging made of blankets and horsehide, and their own ingenuity, they put together a brigantine at a point on the Coca River which they named El Barco—The Boat. Orellana was put in command of the party, and accompanied by Fray Gaspar de Carvajal, who wrote a magnificent description of the hazardous voyage, and sixty men, he sailed down the river, having arranged to meet Pizarro in twelve days. This was the last the expedition saw of Orellana or the boat. Whether he missed Pizarro at the appointed rendezvous, or whether the rebel which lay so near the surface of most of the conquistadors led him to decide to make discoveries on his own has never been determined. (Gonzalo Pizarro brought charges of treason against him, but the Spanish courts exonerated Orellana.) The Coca led them into the Napo, and this in turn into the Marañón, which they followed through months of hunger, skirmishes with hostile Indians, and navigational difficulties of every sort until they came upon the greatest river they had ever beheld, to which they gave the name of Amazon because of the glimpse they caught of what they believed to be women warriors like those of classic antiquity. Finally, some eight months after they had set out, they entered the Atlantic Ocean through the river's mouth near the present-day Pará. They had navigated the river from its extreme upper waters to the open sea, the first white men ever to have made the journey, possibly the first men.

Historians are unable to agree on the baffling figure of Lope de Aguirre. In the opinion of some he was a madman or an unprincipled, evil being; others see in him a forerunner of American independence, for he flouted the authority of Philip II, and in a defiant letter addressed to him upheld the right of the new lands to govern themselves. He was one of those who in 1559 accompanied Pedro de Ursua on another search for El Dorado. The party sailed through the Huallaga River into the Marañón. Before long Lope de Aguirre by his treachery and guile had sowed dissension and created disaffection among the members of the expedition. He murdered Pedro de Ursua, took command of the enterprise himself, and proceeded down the Marañón into the Amazon. His band of followers styled themselves "Marañones" after the river they had navigated. Instead of continuing to the Atlantic by way of the Amazon they reached it by following the Casiquiare and the streams of the Orinoco system, then descended on Venezuela, plundering and killing as they went. The king's authority, however, was strong and relentless, and this rebel band was finally surrounded and defeated by a Spanish force. Many of his men had already deserted Aguirre, appalled in part by his cruelty, and in part by the thought of the fate that awaited them as rebels. He was encircled and shot down in the house where he barricaded himself, after first stabbing to death his daughter who had accompanied him to prevent her falling into the hands of his enemies. "Poor shooting," he said of the first bullet which missed him. "A good shot," he said of the next, as he fell mortally wounded.

It is around this turbulent river that the existence of the *cholos* of Calemar centers, which Alegría has described in this spirited, colorful, tender book. The river is their link to the world and the source of their livelihood. Upon it they travel in their work as boatmen, transporting passengers, cattle, carrying the products of their lush land to market and fairs, where they also find their diversions, their sweethearts, and have their encounters with the representatives of the law, always an unpleasant experience. For instead of the equitable justice of their ancestors—when each community was a link in the chain of authority reaching to the throne of the Inca, and everyone's duties and rights were es-

tablished and safeguarded—for centuries, and especially since the country's independence, the government has
existed only to interfere with their time-honored ways,
to tax them, to conscript them for military service, to
side with their oppressors, and, when they rebelled, to
hunt them down as malefactors.

All this which is adumbrated in *The Golden Serpent*
becomes more explicit in Alegría's second novel *The
Hungry Dogs,* which narrates the life of the herders of
the uplands, and achieves epic proportions in *Broad
and Alien Is the World.* But unlike the protagonists of
the latter, the boatmen of Calemar are not Indians;
they are *cholos,* of mixed Spanish and Indian blood,
and to the fatalism and patient resignation of the Indian they bring the self-reliance and aggressiveness of
their Spanish ancestors. With only their fragile rafts of
balsa wood, and their skill and courage, they ride the
mighty river as though it were a horse they were breaking, meeting its every mood, outwitting its treacherous
currents, shooting its rapids, matching its wiliness with
their own. "What a feeble little structure, the raft,
poised upon the roaring waters as on danger itself. It
carries the life of the man of the Marañón valleys on it,
and he stakes it as on the toss of a coin." They hurl
defiance at it in their song:

> River Marañón, let me cross,
> You are strong and powerful,
> You never forgive.
> River Marañón, I have to cross,
> You have your waters,
> I, my heart.

These are the words of stout-hearted men the world
over; they recall those of that "steel-drivin' " man, John
Henry, who swore that:

> 'Fore he'd let the steam drill beat him down
> He'd die wid his hammer in his hand.

And the adversary commands their respect and admiration. "There's a brave *cholo*," says Lucas the narrator on one occasion to Don Matías, who has lost a son to the river. "The old man turned toward me, fixing me with a look that came from centuries past. 'So is the river. Trying to get the better of it means death for us sometimes. But we don't flee from it because we are men and we have to take things as they come.' "

Not only the river, but the land, too, can be cruel. The young mining engineer who comes out from Lima full of plans for exploiting the mines of the region, and bringing progress to these people whom he looks upon as benighted, yet whose simple, harmonious existence almost beguiles him from his purpose, dies before he can put any of his projects into effect, from the bite of a small, yellow snake, the deadly *intiwaraka,* another golden serpent. As he had been reflecting only moments before his tragic accident: "Here Fate is Nature."

Ciro Alegría is one of the younger of that gifted group of novelists Latin America began to produce in the nineteen-twenties, which includes writers like Ricardo Güiraldes of Argentina, Rómulo Gallegos of Venezuela, José Eustasio Rivera of Colombia, José Lins do Rêgo and Jorge Amado of Brazil, and so many others. Their artistic purpose was to discover and give expression to the reality of their own land and people. This world of the Marañón is one Alegría knows as intimately as do the boatmen of whom he tells. He was born on November 4, 1909, on a ranch in the province of Huamachuco, and when he was three his parents moved to another ranch, one which had belonged to his grandfather, in the same province on the banks of the Marañón. His playmates were the children of people like those he describes in this book; from the servants and ranch hands he heard the tales he narrates in it, the songs he recalls. "I have never forgotten the life I lived there," he writes, "nor my experiences traveling the thin-aired trails of the uplands, the suffering I saw, the tales I heard. My first teachers were my parents,

but the people of all Peru finally molded me in their
own likeness, and made me understand their sorrows,
their joys, their great and overlooked gifts of intelli-
gence and fortitude, their creative ability, their capacity
for endurance." He lived on the ranch until he was
seven, when he was sent to school in the city of Trujillo.
One of his teachers there was César Vallejo, that gifted,
tormented poet who may have communicated to his
equally gifted pupil something of his own impassioned
thirst for social justice.

> Between 1920 and 1924, [observes the Peruvian critic
> Luis Alberto Sánchez] the Peruvian mentality receives
> a series of blows which were to have a deep impact on
> its youthful elements. . . . There came about an intimate
> collaboration between workers and students through the
> people's universities. . . . The Indian became the focal
> point of Peruvian writing. . . . Over and above aesthetic
> considerations, the great concern was with social prob-
> lems. Verse and prose became weapons in the struggle.
> And from this group of young men came the most
> achieved prose writing of the period: a handful of nar-
> ratives with novelistic intent such as *The Golden
> Serpent, The Hungry Dogs, Broad and Alien Is the
> World* by Ciro Alegría. . . .

In 1930 Ciro Alegría entered the University of Trujillo, but his participation in the struggle against the
dictatorship which governed his country prevented him
from continuing his studies. He was one of the founders
of the Aprista party in Trujillo, and on different occasions was imprisoned for his political activities until in
1934 he was exiled to Chile. There he earned a pre-
carious living as a journalist and writer. One of his short
stories, *The Raft,* revised and expanded, became *The
Golden Serpent,* which won first prize in a novel contest sponsored by the publishing house of Nascimento
of Santiago, Chile.

The political strife in which he had engaged, and the
rigors of prison and exile, had undermined his health,
and in 1936 he entered a sanitarium for tubercu-

losis. He remained there for two years. But his convalescence was not a period of idleness; out of it came
his second novel, *The Hungry Dogs*. It, too, received
first prize in a contest sponsored by another publisher
of Santiago. And *Broad and Alien Is the World,* that
panoramic vision of Peru which centers upon the Indian
community of Rumi, its life, its destruction, and the
diaspora of its members, received another.

These three novels, which comprise an epos of Peru,
mark the emergence of the backlands, the provinces,
on the literary scene, dominated until then by Lima, so
spiritually remote from the rest of the country and its
problems. For most of the rural population, Indians
or *cholos,* the beautiful capital from which the country
is governed and where the laws by which they are ruled
are promulgated means little or nothing. As one of the
characters in *Broad and Alien Is the World* says: "Lima
is where the penitentiary is." And it is Alegría speaking
when the Indian Mashe says in *The Hungry Dogs:* "It
is we who are the hungry dogs."

But Alegría is too great a writer to make his protest
against the injustice and neglect under which so many
of his countrymen live mere social tracts whose value
is circumscribed to a moment in history. Like one of
his literary progenitors, the Inca Garcilasso de la Vega,
himself a *cholo,* the son of a conquistador and an Incan
princess, who in his *Royal Commentaries* has left us an
unforgettable picture of the vanished empire of the
Incas, so Alegría's books will stand as a vision of and
tribute to the courage, endurance, and rectitude of his
countrymen when the circumstances which elicited his
protest have disappeared. He has created a world peo-
pled by beings teeming with life, with their sorrows and
joys, their aspirations and defeats, and all suffused with
that poetry which comes from emotion recalled in
tranquillity.

And when progress has spanned the turbulent Marañón with bridges, has dammed and channeled its treach-

erous waters, and the boatmen of Calemar have disappeared, their work done, *The Golden Serpent* will remain as a monument to the days when it ran free and bold, tamed only by brave men.

HARRIET DE ONÍS

Río Piedras
Puerto Rico

—THE END—

SIGNET CLASSICS from Around the World

PLATERO AND I *by Juan Ramon Jimenez*
Translated by William H. and Mary M. Roberts with an
Introduction by William H. Roberts
The delightful tale of a poet and his playful donkey by one
of Spain's great Nobel Prize winning authors.

(#CD17—50¢)

PRIDE AND PREJUDICE *by Jane Austen*
Afterword by Joann Morse
The prejudice of a young lady and the pride of the aristo-
cratic hero make this book a masterpiece of gentle humor.

(#CD82—50¢)

GULLIVER'S TRAVELS *by Jonathan Swift*
Foreword by Marcus Cunliffe
The four classic voyages of Gulliver, which make both a
fascinating fairy tale and a bitter satire. With 30 illustra-
tions by Charles Brock and 5 maps. (#CD15—50¢)

CANDIDE, ZADIG *and Selected Stories by Voltaire*
Newly translated, with an Introduction by Donald Frame
In this fine collection of shorter works, the master of social
commentary employs his ruthless wit to dissect science and
spiritual faith, ethics and legal systems, love and human
vanity. (#CD35—50¢)

ADVENTURES IN THE SKIN TRADE *and Other Stories by Dylan*
Thomas. Afterword by Vernon Watkins
Brilliant and fantastic tales by the great Welsh poet, who
writes of sinners and lovers, nature and madness.

(#CD38—50¢)

ANNA KARENINA *by Leo Tolstoy*
Newly translated, with an Introduction by David Magarshack
Afterword by Franklin Reeve
This classic love story contains the nucleus of Tolstoy's
philosophy. (#CQ34—95¢)

DEAD SOULS *by Nikolai Gogol*
Newly translated by Andrew R. MacAndrew
Foreword by Frank O'Connor
An amusing story about a genial fraud trading in non-existent
serfs. (#CP66—60¢)

LEAVES OF GRASS *by Walt Whitman*
Whitman's enduring testament to a land whose vitality was
the touchstone of his genius. A complete edition.

(#CT23—75¢)

THE TRAVELS OF MARCO POLO
Edited and with an Introduction by Milton Rugoff
The enduring record of Marco Polo's thirty-five years of
fabulous Eastern travel. (#CD97—50¢)

THE INFORMER *by Liam O'Flaherty*
Afterword by Donagh McDonagh
This story of a hunted man who has betrayed his friend to
the enemy presents a harshly realistic picture of Ireland
divided by the Civil War in the 1920's. (#CP80—60¢)

MANON LESCAUT *by Abbe Prevost*
Newly translated with an Introduction by Donald Frame
The first modern "novel of passion," on which the operas
of Massenet and Puccini are based. (#CP96—60¢)

ANTON CHEKHOV: SELECTED STORIES
Foreword by Ernest J. Simmons, translated by Ann Dunnigan
Twenty stories, including a number of early tales which have
never before appeared in English. (#CD37—50¢)

THE BROTHERS KARAMAZOV *by Fyodor Dostoyevsky*
Revised, with a Foreword by Manuel Komroff
Translated by Constance Garnett
The complete and unabridged classic about a passionate and
tragic Russian family. (#CT33—75¢)

1984 *by George Orwell*
Afterword by Erich Fromm
A nightmare projection of a future police state, ruled by
"Big Brother," where "War is Peace" and all values are
transvalued. (#CP100—60¢)

MOBY DICK *by Herman Melville*
Afterword by Denham Sutcliffe
The great epic novel of man's struggle with evil, told in
terms of Captain Ahab's search for the great white whale.
(#CT47—75¢)

TO OUR READERS

If your dealer does not have the SIGNET and MENTOR books
you want, you may order them by mail enclosing the list price
plus 5¢ a copy to cover mailing. If you would like our complete
catalog, please request it by postcard. The New American
Library of World Literature, Inc., P.O. Box 2310, Grand
Central Station, New York 17, New York.